Katherine is dumbfounded when Otis asks her about a concert.

"Concert?"

"Yes." Otis looked at her quizzically. "Surely you won't mind that I make mention of this in front of your friend Christopher, since he is certain to be included in your plans."

"Uh, of course."

"Oh well, perhaps you are not aware, Katherine. Miranda said in her correspondence to me that I must visit Maryland some time—"

"She said that?" No wonder he had decided to make the trip.

"Why, yes." He continued undeterred. "And she said that when I did, all of you would put on a concert. Wouldn't that be splendid?"

"Uh, splendid indeed."

"I certainly hope that event comes about. She suggested that I might add a song or two on the piano. I've been practicing several of my favorite tunes ever since her missive arrived."

"How sweet of you," Katherine noted.

"Yes, how sweet." Christopher didn't sound as sincere. He crossed his arms.

If Otis was bothered by Christopher's aside, he didn't let them know. "Miranda also mentioned that your church will be putting on a talent show later this month. Perhaps the concert among friends will be good practice for that event as well."

"Indeed." Katherine hadn't given the talent show much thought. Now Otis was recruiting her to take part.

FICTION

TAMELA HANCOCK MURRAY is an award-winning, best-selling author living in northern Virginia. She and her husband of over twenty years are blessed with two daughters. Their first, an honors student, is a college freshman at Tamela's alma mater. Their second, a student at Christian school, keeps them busy with church activities and AWANA. Tamela loves to take mini vacations with her family, and she also enjoys reading and Bible study. Visit Tamela's Web site: www.tamelahancockmurray.com

Books by Tamela Hancock Murray

HEARTSONG PRESENTS
HP213—Picture of Love
HP408—Destinations
HP453—The Elusive Mr. Perfect
HP501—Thrill of the Hunt
HP544—A Light among Shadows
HP568—Loveswept
HP598—More Than Friends
HP616—The Lady and the Cad
HP621—Forever Friends
HP639—Love's Denial
HP663—Journeys

The Ruse

Tamela Hancock Murray

Heartsong Presents

To the real Mr. and Mrs. Christopher Bagley

A note from the Author:
I love to hear from my readers! You may correspond with me by writing:

Tamela Hancock Murray
Author Relations
PO Box 721
Uhrichsville, OH 44683

ISBN 1-59310-944-X

THE RUSE

All scripture quotations are taken from the King James Version of the Bible.

All of the characters and events in this book are fictitious. Any resemblance to actual persons, living or dead, or to actual events is purely coincidental.

Our mission is to publish and distribute inspirational products offering exceptional value and biblical encouragement to the masses.

PRINTED IN THE U.S.A.

prologue

Katherine Jones looked over the letter she had just penned to Otis Rath, a brave sailor fighting in the war against the Spaniards. Despite Otis's noteworthy war record and adventures at sea, she found writing to Otis much more difficult than writing to her childhood friend Christopher Bagley. Her pen flowed with no effort over the paper as she told Christopher, who was away at agricultural college, all about the week's events. They knew the same people, had been taught by the same teacher, and had attended the same church when Christopher was home. He understood her. But Otis was a stranger.

"What did you write?" Miranda Henderson asked from across the kitchen table.

Miranda kept up a lively correspondence with her cousin Matthew in the army, but Katherine was writing to a man she had never met as a favor to her beloved uncle. After the first few sentences, Katherine struggled. What could she tell Otis?

Still holding the ivory-colored rag paper, Katherine leaned her chin on her palm. "Oh, I don't know what to write. Otis and I have no acquaintances in common, and nothing exciting seems to happen here."

Miranda snatched Katherine's letter and read over it. "What makes you think he would want to read this? Who cares that you gathered more eggs than usual this week? Or what the preacher said last Sunday? Unless you think Otis is some kind of heathen, and you're looking for a convert." Miranda sniffed.

"Christopher doesn't seem to mind such news."

"That's different. You've known him all your life."

"Precisely." Katherine sighed. "Maybe I never should have agreed to correspond with someone I've never met."

"Especially if your main purpose for writing is to bring him to the faith."

"No, that's not my reason. Besides, Otis says he loves the Lord. And of course I never would use war correspondence to gain a convert unless God gave me a clear leading to do so."

"And He hasn't." Miranda scooted the letter across the table back at Katherine as though it was better suited for the trash bin than the postman. "I say that if you never want to hear from your sailor again, just keep giving him a Sunday school report."

"If my letter is so boring, then you must know how to write a most entertaining missive. So tell me, what are you writing to your cousin in the army?"

"I'm glad you asked." Miranda smiled, held up the letter, and read aloud:

Dear Matthew,

This has proven to be the most exciting week I have experienced since the commencement of our correspondence! Much to the delight of the Ladies' Horsewomen's Club, I earned a blue ribbon to add to my growing collection, for my equestrian skills in jumping hurdles. My mare, Ash, was in fine form as usual, guided with my gentle but experienced and firm hand. The trophy I won is a handsome one and looks well on my bookshelf.

I have been working on my needlework to enter in the fair. The sampler, a colorful example of fine work, is almost ready.

I am sure it will be recognized with yet another ribbon to add to my collection.

My room is so filled with trophies and ribbons that I do believe we'll soon need to add yet another room to the house to hold them all! But no number of accolades I can earn with my puny endeavors can ever compare to the many medals you deserve for fighting for your country each and every day. Putting yourself in harm's way is ever so brave. My heart flutters in fear to think about the danger you face. The members of the fairer sex and the men left on the home front who are unable to go in your stead are all so grateful for your courage and sacrifice.

To show my friendly and familial devotion, I am enclosing a small lock of my hair. When you look at this little memento, remember me, your dear cousin, as I remember you in fond kinship for your bravery.

> *Yours most sincerely,*
> *Miranda*

Katherine shook her head upon hearing such hyperbole. "I do declare, that is some letter."

"Entertaining, is it not?"

"It certainly does detail your recent accomplishments. No doubt your cousin finds such news fascinating. But I haven't earned any ribbons lately, and I'm not one to pour on the praise like you are, Miranda. Such writing comes easily to you but not to me. It's just not in my nature."

"Maybe you should follow my example and make it part of your nature, then."

"Maybe I should." Katherine stared at the words she had written to Otis, but her mind was too filled with woe to comprehend them. "Maybe I'm not called to cheer up a sailor.

I should concede defeat." She looked at Miranda. "Although even if my letter was the most trite in the world, Otis would have bragging rights since he'd be getting mail. Doesn't that count for something?"

"Bragging rights, eh?" Miranda snapped her fingers. "Then why don't you give your sailor something to brag about?"

"What do you mean?"

"You've sent him a portrait of yourself, haven't you?"

"Yes, the best one I have." Katherine nodded.

"The one of you in the white lace dress?"

"That's the one."

"Good. Then all the other fellows know he's writing to a lovely brunette with big eyes. Now all you have to do is to make yourself seem just a little more. . .exciting."

"Miranda! Are you telling me to lie?"

"Of course not." She tapped her fingers ever so lightly on the table. "Just embellish a little. What's the harm?"

Katherine leaned back in her chair in a failed effort to separate herself from Miranda and her suggestion. "What a terrible Christian I would be if I pretended to be someone I'm not. I can't. Not even to cheer up a brave military man."

"Hmm. Well, maybe I can change your mind."

Katherine shook her head. "Never." She sealed the envelope. "If Otis doesn't want to read about the sermon, that's fine by me. He can stop writing, then."

Miranda didn't say another word. Then why did the look on her face leave Katherine wondering…and worrying?

one

Washington County, Maryland, 1901

Though Otis had been honorably discharged from the service, Katherine's correspondence with him hadn't diminished one iota. If anything, his hints of admiration of her only increased with time.

So when a letter written in a fine hand appeared in the family's stack of mail one Tuesday morning, she felt no surprise. Only when she studied its contents did she sit down in a kitchen chair.

Otis was planning a visit. He would be arriving the next day! Katherine let out a gasp.

"Is that a letter from the sailor?" Katherine's ten-year-old sister asked, looking up from the comics section of a newspaper.

"Yes, Betsy."

"What's wrong?"

"Nothing."

"Then why do you seem surprised?" Betsy's brown eyes took on a heightened glint.

"His news is unexpected, that's why. He's coming for a visit."

It was Betsy's turn to let out a breath. "Oh! How exciting! I wonder if he wrote me, too."

Katherine flipped through the pile of mail. "As a matter of fact, he did." She handed her a white envelope bearing Otis's precise script.

"Goodie!" Betsy ripped open the letter and drew out a prize. "Look! He sent me a bookmark!"

"Oh, how lovely. I know he's proud that you are reading so well now."

Betsy began reading her missive from Otis.

Katherine interrupted with a thought. "Oh, I must tell Mother." She rushed upstairs, where Mother was folding laundry.

The older woman turned to her. "What is it, Katherine? You're running around like there's a fire, only you look too happy for anything to be terribly wrong."

"Oh, no, nothing is wrong. Indeed, everything is just right!"

"Like Goldilocks in the fairy tale, eh?" Mother teased.

Katherine clasped her hands. "You could say that." She rocked back and forth with glee. "Otis is coming from South Carolina to visit us!"

Mother gasped. "He's coming all that way?"

"Yes. Can you believe it?"

Mother thought for a moment. "As a matter of fact, I can. You've been writing to him for quite some time, and I don't think the correspondence would have lasted so long after the war unless he was at least a mite sweet on you."

Blushing, Katherine took a sudden interest in the starched curtains framing her parents' bedroom window. "I don't know about that, but I do look forward to his visit."

"When is he due to arrive?"

"Tomorrow!"

Mother's expression went from pleased to alarmed. "Tomorrow? Why, we'll hardly have time to prepare any food. And we must air out Ralph's room for him. The sheets are clean, but it might not hurt to put fresh ones on the bed for Otis all the same." Mother hurried to place a pile of unmentionables in her dresser drawer. "My, but we must start right away. Get a rag and wipe the furniture in Ralph's room real good now, and dust everything downstairs, too. Especially in the formal parlor. You hear?"

"Yes, ma'am." Katherine wasn't worried. Mother was in the habit of keeping her house clean enough for company on a moment's notice.

"Oh, I do wish we had time to polish everything."

"We just polished for spring cleaning. I think everything looks fine."

"To your eyes, maybe. But you're accustomed to how things look around here. He'll be seeing everything for the first time. Oh, I wish he'd given us more notice!"

"I have a feeling he wants to see us the way we really are. I think we're pretty presentable most of the time."

Mother laughed. "I hope so. All the same, I would have appreciated more time to spruce up." She snapped her fingers. "Oh, I thought of something else."

Katherine tried not to grimace at the thought of even more work. "Yes, ma'am?"

"I'll need you to sweep the floors after you dust."

"I will." At the rate Mother was doling out assignments, Katherine feared the afternoon would melt into evening before she finished. "Um, Mother?"

"Yes?"

"After I do those chores, may I run to Miranda's for a spell? I promise to keep my visit quick, and I'll be glad to do anything else you need upon my return."

"Oh, all right. I suppose so. But make it quick, now. And tell Betsy to come see me. I'll be needing her help, too."

"Yes, ma'am."

Katherine's little sister was just about to escape to the

outdoors when Katherine returned downstairs.

"Mother wants to see you," Katherine informed her.

The brown-haired girl wrinkled her nose. "She wants me to do more chores, doesn't she?"

"That's a good guess. But I'm doing my part, too," Katherine assured, holding up a dust rag. "I've got to cover the whole house. And I've got to sweep, too." Katherine knew those facts would console her sister, who hated sweeping with a passion.

"I wonder what she wants me to do."

"I don't know, but the sooner you start, the sooner you'll be done. Oh, and I'll be going to Miranda's as soon as I dust and sweep, but I'll be back to do more chores. I'd like to bake a pie tonight if I have time."

"Mother will want me to fetch the preserves from the cellar, then." Betsy's voice brightened. "Oh, and tell Miranda I said hello. Did she get her new charm yet?"

"What charm?"

"She was supposed to get a new charm for her bracelet. An aunt was going to send her a souvenir from her trip to Egypt."

"Egypt!" Katherine couldn't imagine visiting somewhere so exotic. "No, she hasn't said anything yet."

"She's hoping for a new charm, but her aunt didn't promise. It might be something else. But you can ask her." Betsy sighed. "I hope I can have a bracelet as pretty as that one someday."

Katherine grinned. "Maybe someday you will."

A short while later as she finished her dusting and sweeping, Katherine glanced at the kitchen wall clock. It told her that Miranda was likely to be occupied with her own weekly dusting. "I won't bother Miranda if I drop in. I can talk to her as she works," she muttered to herself. She slid out the back door, an early summer breeze tickling her face.

After bicycling across the road, Katherine found herself

moments later visiting the Henderson house, a large brick affair complete with a carriage house and separate guesthouse.

She found Miranda dusting her family's formal parlor, a much larger room than the modest area of the Joneses' house.

Miranda stopped her chore and urged Katherine to take a seat beside her on the velvet sofa. "I have to say, you seem excited."

Katherine sat—but not still. "I am! You'll never guess what news I have!"

"What?"

She took Miranda's hands in hers. "Otis is coming here for a visit!"

Miranda took her hands out of Katherine's. "After all this time?"

"Yes. Can you believe it?" Katherine had to suppress herself from clapping.

"No. Yes. I mean, I don't know." Miranda embraced her. "Oh, Katherine! This is wonderful! Do you think he means to court you?"

"I—I don't know. Perhaps." She averted her gaze to a blue Oriental rug.

"How splendid!" But her friend's exuberance only lasted a moment before her mouth opened into an uncertain circle. "Uh oh."

Katherine froze. "Uh oh? What do you mean?"

It was Miranda's turn to avert her glance. She studied her hands. Even though Miranda was merely engaged in household drudgery, she nevertheless wore her ubiquitous gold charm bracelet that Betsy had mentioned. Miranda also wore two rings. One was set with a sapphire and the other with a pearl and two diamonds barely visible to the human eye. "I'm afraid there's something I have to tell you."

Katherine sat beside Miranda. Fear engulfed her, but she had to know the reason for Miranda's sudden change of mood. "What?"

Miranda took a minute to compose herself before she spoke. "You know how I think—in fact I know—you're a fine woman. Any man would be fortunate to court you."

Such flattery from the self-absorbed Miranda pricked Katherine with suspicion. She let her friend continue unabated.

"And I know how you've always wanted to play the banjo and harp, and that you wish you had kept up with your dancing skills, that you long to play the piano like a graduate of Juilliard, and that you wish you were as good with horses as I am."

Katherine sighed. "Yes. That would be nice, wouldn't it? But alas, it is only a dream. And I certainly don't see what this has to do with Otis's visit." An uneasy feeling overcame her, leaving her with a sudden desire to flee.

Miranda kept her riveted. "Yet you are so accomplished in your own right. You sew a fine seam, and your cooking is rivaled only by your dear mother's."

"You're making me blush. Please, don't flatter me." Her friend's compliments, while she knew them to be sincere, alarmed her.

"But it's true! And Otis should appreciate all those fine things about you. And he'll appreciate you even more when you show him how well you play the harp, ride a horse, play the piano, and dance."

"I beg your pardon?" Katherine felt the color run off from her face. "When I show him what?"

Miranda cleared her throat. "All the things you said you always wanted to be."

"But Miranda! I only shared those thoughts with you

in confidence. Of course it would be wonderful to be so accomplished, but developing those skills takes work. Years of work. I haven't made the time or effort to earn the right to claim any of those talents. And I never would."

"I know you wouldn't."

"So. . ."

"So I—well, you know I was writing to Otis, too."

"Yes, you kept that no secret. And he is a free man. He can write to anyone he likes. But I still don't see the connection you seem to be trying to make."

"Otis never detailed our correspondence to you?"

Katherine shrugged. "I see no reason why he owed me any explanation about your letter exchange. As I said, he's a free man, and I trust you as a friend."

Miranda blanched. "Your trust was not misplaced. Not exactly. In fact, I said nothing but flattering things about you."

"You talked about me? I can't imagine why. Not after you chastised me about my letters being a bore. Whatever could you have said about me that he would find enthralling?" An unwanted thought struck her mind. "Unless. . .oh, Miranda, you didn't make up wild stories about imaginary accomplishments of mine, did you?"

When her friend didn't rush to reassure Katherine, she knew they were both in trouble.

"Miranda!"

Miranda grimaced and then lifted her finger in a victorious way. "Never fear. I didn't exaggerate. Not much."

A groan flew from Katherine's lips. "Why did you feel the need to exaggerate at all?"

"Well. . .I wanted to cheer him up. And believe you me, I did! I told him how wonderful you are and about your many talents," said the matchmaking friend.

"And about how brave he is, no doubt."

"True."

"That I don't mind. All of our military men are courageous and daring. But why did you have to make up stories about me?"

"I didn't. Exactly." Miranda blushed. "Well, maybe I did. I just wanted him to like you even more than he already did. You. . .you do like him, don't you?"

"Well, yes, but I didn't mean for you to intervene on my behalf."

"I meant well, you know."

"I know." Katherine summoned her patience. Miranda possessed a kind heart, but her interpretations of right and wrong were often painted gray. "But surely you knew that the truth would come to light one day."

Miranda drummed her fingers on the edge of the sofa and studied them. "Looks like 'one day' has finally arrived. But I wouldn't worry if I were you. Once Otis sees you and how charming and accomplished you really are, he's certain to love you just as much as I do. Even more so."

Katherine tried not to be too harsh in her admonishment. "Oh, Miranda, you always did love a good romance. But honestly, you never should have tried to lead Otis to believe I'm anything more than I really am. He's sure to feel let down when he sees me in person." Katherine felt her heart descend into the depths of her stomach in disappointment.

Miranda let out a horrified breath. "No, you mustn't let that happen. You have to convince Otis that you possess all the talents I mentioned."

"You mean convince him that I can actually do all the things that have only been a fantastic notion for me all these years?"

"Of course. How much time do we have?"

Fear struck her. "None. He'll be here tomorrow."

"Tomorrow!" Darkness cast a shadow on Miranda's face, but she soon composed her lips into a sunny smile. "Well, we'll just have to get working on you right away."

"No, Miranda, we've got to confess the truth to Otis. We can cast our bread upon the waters and pray for his pardon."

"No! No, you can't. How will that make me look in front of him? He's bound to pass judgment on me and tell all my friends. I'll look like a fool." Miranda's breathing became noticeable.

"I don't think so."

"That is one place where we disagree, Katherine, and I don't want to take a chance. Please, since you are my dearest friend in the world, you have to help me. Why, if anyone found out I had embellished the truth, I would just lie down and die."

"Oh, Miranda, you exaggerate."

"See? You're already saying it. You're calling me a liar, even in casual conversation."

"No, that's not what I meant."

Miranda withdrew a lace handkerchief and brought it up to her eyes. "I only did it for you. I only want you to be happy. And you were, weren't you? Otis is very fond of you. Fond enough to visit. Maybe even fond enough to court you."

"But I don't want his love if it's based on a lie."

"It won't be. I promise."

"I'm not so sure—"

Miranda sniffled. "Oh, you must not say anything to Otis or anyone else. I promise I'll help you. I'll do anything. Please keep my secret. If people think I'm a liar, my reputation would be ruined, and I'll never be able to find anyone to marry me. Ever. My future would be dismal. My whole life would be nothing but a shambles. No one, male or female, would trust me again. I'd be destined to spinsterhood. Please don't ask me to be a spinster forever, Katherine! I'd rather die!" Miranda had worked herself up into sobs, her blond curls bobbing up and down as her shoulders shook, and she blew her nose into the cloth. "Please, I beg you not to force me to be a spinster!"

Katherine knew she was asking Miranda no such thing, but her friend's antics stunned her into silence. Miranda, always one for the dramatic, nevertheless accepted as unvarnished truth every word she uttered. She believed that Katherine would ruin her life if she let on to anyone that any word bearing a shade of dishonesty had ever escaped Miranda's tinted lips. Katherine's heart stung her chest with pain upon seeing her friend's distress.

"Oh, please, Katherine? Can't you just let on that you possess all these talents, just for a while? After all, he won't be here long, will he?" Miranda blew her nose once more.

"He didn't give an exact time. I don't suppose he could leave his business more than a couple of weeks at the most."

A little smile curved Miranda's lips. "Good. Well, if it's too much for you to convince him entirely, maybe you can hint that you are quite accomplished, just as I said."

"You have more confidence than I do." Katherine's mind whirred at the thought of her plight.

"There's a reason for my confidence. Never fear, Katherine. I have a plan."

two

That afternoon, Christopher stopped by the Joneses' house to return a cup of sugar his mother had borrowed from Mrs. Jones. Happy to see her friend, Katherine poured them both lemonade and suggested they sit under the oaks in the backyard for a time. Christopher seemed all too happy to take Katherine up on her suggestion, a fact that gladdened her. A nagging thought that if Otis came courting, she wouldn't be able to visit with Christopher with such spontaneity anymore shot through her mind, but she dismissed such dreary thoughts.

"I have good news," she told him well into their visit.

"Oh?" His blue eyes took on an interested light, and he leaned toward her slightly in his wicker chair.

"Remember Otis?"

"Otis. Yes." The excitement left his voice. "The sailor. Are you still writing to him?"

"Yes. I told you that."

"You did? How about that."

Katherine tried to ignore his lack of enthusiasm. Christopher usually wasn't so forgetful. Why was he being like this? She made a deliberate effort to fill her voice with life. "Well, you shouldn't mind. After all, you always told me how much you appreciated my letters when you were away at school."

"Yes, but that's different." He winced.

"I don't see how—"

"Never mind. So what's your news?" Christopher's mouth

19

straightened. He didn't look happy.

Katherine hesitated but pressed on. "He's coming for a visit."

Christopher's eyes widened then narrowed. "Is that so? How about that. When?"

"Tomorrow."

"So soon?" He leaned back in his chair. "You seem relaxed about the whole thing."

"I've already swept and dusted, and with Mother and Betsy working along with me, there's not much else left to do, really. He can take us as we are. Well"—she felt her face flush—"sort of."

"What do you mean, sort of?"

Katherine paused. After taking in a breath to prepare herself, she revealed Miranda's plan to Christopher.

"Miranda has convinced you to do what?" Christopher's blue eyes lit with surprise and anguish.

His obvious disapproval left her disconcerted. "I know it sounds wild, but she only got in this mess because she was trying to help me. Now I feel obligated to help her get out of it."

"I don't think he'll ever believe it, Katherine. I think you should tell him right away, the minute he arrives. You don't want him to be disappointed, do you?"

"No. But I won't disappoint him. I've always wanted to be a skilled horsewoman, a ballerina, a banjo player, a harmonica player, and a harpist. I'll just have to accomplish all these skills a little earlier, that's all." She brightened. "That gives me an idea. You're accomplished on the banjo."

"Yes?" His tone revealed how leery he felt.

"So will you help me? Please?"

"How?"

"Your part is easy. Just teach me one tune on the banjo. That's all."

"One tune is not going to convince him that you are accomplished on the instrument." Christopher settled in his seat like an immovable object and swirled the melting ice in his glass.

"Miranda promised to change the subject before he can ask me to play something else."

Christopher didn't answer right away, which gave her hope. But then he shook his head. "I want to help you, but I can't. I just can't. I'm sorry, Katherine. You're on your own this time."

"You can't?" Vexation and hurt crossed her expression. She rose from her chair and took the glass from him. "It was nice to see you, Christopher, but I must bid you good day. You see, I must bake a cherry pie for my visitor."

❧

Christopher watched Katherine walk into her house and slam the back door behind her. He knew everything was not fine. Would it ever be?

The idea that this Otis fellow planned to come in and sweep Katherine off her feet filled him with ire. Christopher had been planning to ask Mr. Jones if he could court Katherine. They had known one another since childhood, so Christopher didn't anticipate a long courtship. He only wanted to be betrothed long enough for Katherine to plan a wedding. Knowing that Katherine didn't want to put on airs, he imagined his bride would want a simple day. A few words uttered by the preacher in front of their closest friends and family, followed by a short reception featuring one of those big tiered cakes that the women liked to bake. Katherine wouldn't demand an elaborate or expensive honeymoon trip, either, although he wanted to give her the best few days of her life. If they married in the fall after the harvest, they could steal away to a nice hotel in Washington, D.C., perhaps. They could see the monuments and take in a little history. The thought brought a smile to his lips.

All too soon, he recalled why these plans would have to be delayed. Perhaps they would have to be forgotten. The idea that Katherine might never be his speared his heart.

What had happened to Katherine, the sweet girl he knew and loved? Why was she letting Miranda wrap her up in a scheme to fool a correspondent she didn't even know? Well, she hardly knew. He balled his hands into fists and relaxed them.

Father in heaven, I pray for patience.

As soon as he sent up the silent prayer, Christopher knew the answer. Katherine was sweet. Too sweet. Which was why Miranda could put on a few tears and melt Katherine's resolve. Miranda was taking advantage of their friendship, and he didn't like it. Not one bit.

Patience, Lord. Please.

The ride back to the Bagley farm seemed to take longer than usual. Once he arrived, he took a moment to compose himself before he went into the kitchen. "Christopher, you're late for supper," Mother pointed out the instant he entered.

Christopher shut the back door so it thumped to a close with a gentle rap. He didn't mind his mother's reprimand. Though her tone was always serious, he knew her firm hand was a sign of her desire to make sure he never wavered from conducting himself in the way a country gentleman should.

"Your daddy's already getting me another load of wood for the stove."

Guilt visited him as he realized he could have brought his mother fresh fuel for the fire if he had arrived a few moments earlier. "Yes, ma'am. I didn't mean to be late." He looked beside the stove and noted the sparse state of the wood box. After he had returned home from college, he soon realized his parents expected him to resume his chores. Upon reflection, he surmised that such an expectation seemed fair. His brothers and sister had left home to marry in past years, leaving Grandpa and his parents at home. Long past his sixtieth birthday, Grandpa possessed vigor, but he could hardly be expected to perform Christopher's chores.

He glanced at Mother, who was at that moment setting the kitchen table with the everyday dishes painted with blue flowers he had known since childhood.

"Mother, I'll get you a couple of extra loads of wood after supper." He took off the brimmed hat that had protected his head from the warm sun and hung it on the wooden peg beside the door.

"I'll excuse you this time. Just don't make a habit of it. You might have been able to run wild and do as you pleased at school, but you're living by my rules now," Mother reminded him as she set a spoon on the table. "Now get washed up." She tilted her head toward the basin as though Christopher no longer remembered its location despite the fact it hadn't changed in his lifetime.

He suppressed a chuckle. "Yes, ma'am."

"So how are the Joneses?"

"Fine. Just fine. Mrs. Jones thanks you for the return of the sugar, even though she said you didn't need to bother."

Mother nodded.

"Is that beef stew I smell?" While Christopher wanted to know, he also welcomed a way to distract his mother.

"Sure is. So did you see Katherine?"

So much for distractions. "Yes, ma'am."

"And what is the latest news with her?"

"Not much. Her correspondent from South Carolina is coming for a visit."

Mother stopped stirring the stew long enough to look him in the eye. "Her correspondent? That sailor you told me about?"

"Yes, ma'am."

"I would have thought she would have stopped with that letter-writing nonsense after the war was over. I hope he doesn't think he can just swoop in here and take over everything."

"I don't know what his plans are, Mother." He sat down with a sigh.

Grandpa chose that moment to shuffle into the kitchen. "What plans?"

"Katherine's correspondent is coming for a visit."

"Oh." Grandpa shrugged. "Well, that shouldn't bother you none, Christopher. I doubt he can offer you much competition." He sniffed the air. "I've been waiting for some of that good stew, and I think I smell your yeast rolls cooking, too, don't I, Daughter?"

Mother nodded. "Yes, Papa."

"Good." Without fanfare, Grandpa sat down at his regular place at the table. Christopher judged by his slow movements and lethargic expression that he had just awakened from his afternoon nap.

Mother set a pan of rolls on the coolest part of the stove. The light brown tops were shiny. He had often watched her brush the bread with beaten egg whites. He didn't know much about cooking, but he supposed that extra step was what resulted in the sheen that made the bread look so appetizing. Obviously she had prepared the bread to her usual perfection.

Christopher heard Daddy kicking the bottom of the back door, a sure sign that he had a pile of chopped wood in his arms and couldn't open it himself. He hurried to assist him.

"Sorry, Daddy. I was planning to get some wood after supper."

Daddy released wood from his arms and let the split logs fall into the metal box. "You can take a turn next time." He smiled.

"Yes, sir." Christopher returned to his seat. The milk in Grandpa's glass looked appealing. He poured himself a glass from the green pitcher Mother had left on the table.

Mother set a bowl of stew in front of Grandpa. Christopher observed Grandpa watching the steam rise and watched in amusement as the older man surveyed the food, a satisfied expression on his face.

Christopher didn't listen to the banter of the others as he ate his beef stew, bread, and ice-cold milk. All he could think about was Katherine and how they had corresponded while he completed his studies at Maryland Agricultural College. His plans to court Katherine were dashed when Katherine asked him to participate in the ruse Miranda had cooked up to fool the war hero.

He didn't know which part of his visit to Katherine's upset him more—the request for him to help her fool this Otis fellow or her apparent attachment to the sailor who was important enough that she wanted to make him think the best of her.

Otis hadn't seemed so threatening when he was safely tucked away—far away—on a navy ship. Once he was discharged, he seemed so distant in another state way down south. But now that he was coming to see them, well that was another story. If only Christopher could put a stop to the visit!

But what should stop Otis from visiting? Christopher knew he had no right to dictate to Katherine with whom she chose to correspond or if and when that person should come up to Maryland.

What a fool he had been not to realize that the correspondence could evolve into romantic notions. Not that he blamed

Otis. Who wouldn't take a chance in flirting with a woman of such beauty? He thought about Katherine's big brown eyes, smooth skin, and glossy dark brown hair. The image of her face had kept him motivated at college when he felt lonely and wanted nothing more than to go back to the home he knew and loved. Now that he had returned home, apparently the situation had changed, and he could no longer depend on resuming his relationship with the woman he had loved since he was a boy.

"Another glass of milk, Christopher?"

He lurched back into reality. "Oh. No thanks, Mother."

She set the pitcher back on the table and sent him a look that told him he was being too quiet. He could only be grateful for her discretion in not prying. Spooning into a square of warm bread pudding laced with cinnamon and bulging with raisins, Christopher allowed his thoughts to wander to Katherine and her dilemma.

How could Katherine have developed a love for this interloper rather than him? If anyone's correspondence should have developed into mutual love, it should have been the one they had shared. Christopher and Katherine had exchanged letters when he was away studying. He hadn't written flowery words or poetry to her. He had hoped she had some idea about the feelings he harbored for her. But judging from her actions, she did not. If only he had made his feelings known! Maybe then this usurper wouldn't have proven to be such a temptation for the only woman he had ever loved. The only woman he could love.

Lord, why is Katherine tempted away from me? What can I do? I don't want to lose her. I don't think my life would be as happy without her.

His chest tightened in anger even as he tidied up his hands with a napkin. Maybe all this was happening because the Lord knew Katherine wasn't right for him. As a friend, perhaps. But not as a wife. How could she ask him to help her fool Otis, a stranger she'd never met?

Christopher set his spoon in the empty dish, wishing he hadn't been thinking such dark thoughts so he could have enjoyed the delicious treat. He noticed that Mother had held back two extra desserts for later, but he nursed no hope of enjoying either. Grandpa was sure to sneak them both before the next day. Sighing, Christopher rocked back in his chair so only the back two legs balanced on the floor.

"Christopher!" Mother's voice cut through the air. "Where are your manners? You're liable to put a hole in the floor rocking back like that."

He set the front two legs back on the wide plank floor, making sure to be gentle with the motion lest he dent the wood. "Yes, ma'am."

Still, his mother's worries about her floor were the least of his. He couldn't imagine how the little bit of rocking he might do could ruin pine floors that had seen his parents through twenty-nine years of marriage. The thought made him realize how lucky they were.

If only he had spoken up to Katherine sooner! Then he could have looked at the whole scenario with amusement. Katherine had always wanted to dance ballet, ride horses at an expert level, and play the harp, harmonica, and banjo. Everyone knew it. But for Miranda to tell Otis such fantasies! And for what? Some man who didn't care about Katherine. At least, not as much as he did. And always had.

Christopher knew that Katherine never would have written such embellishments on her own; she was much too sweet for that. But now that her so-called friend had written Otis that she had mastered so many accomplishments, Katherine was in a bind. He could understand why Katherine didn't want to embarrass Miranda even though she deserved it. Yet the fact that Katherine didn't want to get her friend in trouble only made him love her all the more.

He wanted to send up a silent prayer that she would make a fool of herself. Such action would serve her right for agreeing to make that poor sailor think she could do so many things. After all, she was a consummate cook and an expert in the domestic arts. Those talents were far more important to the enjoyment of everyday life than being an expert horsewoman or playing the harmonica and banjo. But she couldn't see that, he supposed.

Temptation to pray for her downfall prodded him.

Lord. . .

Lord, please make Katherine see that she doesn't need to change a thing about herself. Help her to see her true value, that she doesn't need to put on a show to protect a friend. I know her good-heartedness is what got her into this mess, Lord. I ask Thee to protect her in these coming weeks. In the name of Thy Son, amen.

He knew the prayer he uttered in silence was far more loving than his original thoughts. Even better, the peace he felt in his heart told him that he meant every word. Whatever happened during her correspondent's visit would be in God's hands. He would have to make himself content in that knowledge.

three

The next day, Katherine heard the sound of horses' hooves thudding and carriage wheels turning against the dirt road leading to their house. The impending arrival of a guest left her with a sense of anticipation and fear. The visitor had to be Otis. She peered through white cotton curtains adorning her bedroom window and watched the hired carriage, drawn by two black and brown horses, come to a stop. It shook as its occupant moved to the side and then disembarked.

Otis emerged. Katherine remembered the small portrait she possessed of him and had always hoped it was not an image that flattered its subject too greatly. As his picture promised, he had coal black hair and dark eyes, but his complexion looked much paler than she anticipated. And he appeared to be shorter than she had envisioned. Instead of the hulking war hero she expected, he seemed slight, though he bore a paunch. In a moment of guilt, she set back the curtain. Though spying wasn't her habit, realizing he wasn't quite as she anticipated ahead of time would keep her from making a face of disappointment or doing something else that might cause embarrassment to him—or to herself.

The thought stirred her to peek once more.

To her surprise, a collie emerged behind him on a leash.

"He brought a dog? I don't remember him mentioning a dog." The animal, though cumbersome in size, looked cute with a coat of long black, white, and tan fur, a pink tongue moving back and forth with his panting. He barked as if to announce his arrival.

Standing beside the carriage, Otis inspected the house, but Katherine couldn't tell from his expression whether or not the two-story white clapboard structure with its black roof and matching shutters met his expectations. She watched him look over the landscape, knowing his gaze would rest upon the lush green lawn that she had run across time and again as a girl. He would also view large, mature trees. She allowed herself a smile when she remembered how often as a child she had climbed those trees, much to her mother's worry.

His gaze wandered to her window. She scooted to the side so he couldn't see her. As soon as he occupied himself with paying the driver, she resumed her observation unencumbered.

He picked up his trunk without huffing, so apparently he was stronger than he appeared. She decided that was good, since he looked as though the slightest breeze could pick him up off his feet and blow him all the way back to Charleston. Katherine couldn't help but notice that compared to Christopher, robust and muscular from years of working his family's farm, Otis looked downright weak.

Christopher! She let out a puff of air so strong that it threatened to move the curtain. She was mad at him. She had to remember that.

Otis approached the porch. Katherine rushed down the stairs and into the kitchen so he wouldn't realize she had been watching him. He would tap the front door knocker, and she would emerge from the room as though she hadn't thought a thing of his impending arrival. Better yet, he might think she was cooking something delicious. As a first impression, such an idea wouldn't hurt.

Katherine had just crossed the threshold when the knocker sounded.

Sitting at the kitchen table, Mother stopped sorting through a jar of buttons long enough to look at the clock. "Is it two o'clock already? That must be your friend. My, but time flies."

"Yes, ma'am."

Katherine's sister, Betsy, grinned. "Katherine's got a beau! Katherine's got a beau!"

"Not true!" Katherine objected.

"Enough of that, Betsy," Mother scolded. "I'd better not catch you saying any such thing again."

"Yes, ma'am." Betsy glanced at the floor.

Katherine wondered if Mother would respond to the second knocking on the door. Mother was quick to put her question to rest. "Well, don't just stand there. Answer the door!"

"Do I look well enough?" Katherine touched the side of her smooth brown chignon. She had selected her Sunday dress to wear for Otis since he would be seeing her in person for the first time. The frock, a bright yellow reminiscent of spring daffodils, complimented her dark hair and olive-toned complexion. Since she and her mother had just sewn the dress from a new pattern the past spring, she felt confident she appeared as fashionable as any of the ladies Otis might know in Charleston.

"Yes, you look very attractive in that dress, and you know it," Mother assured her. "And I see the pink is still in your cheeks from where you pinched them just now."

Katherine blushed, no doubt producing red in her cheeks not unlike the roses in Mother's flower garden.

Mother chuckled. "Such affectations were popular in my day as well. You must really be out to impress your correspondent. Now run along and answer that door. You have accomplished the trick of not appearing too eager, but now you are in danger of making him think we are not at home, or worse, that you are lazy."

"Oh, we can't have that!" Nevertheless, Katherine walked with a dignified gait. In her own letters to Otis, she had portrayed herself as a lady. She was determined that the reality of their visit would match her letters, if not Miranda's exaggerated descriptions. She smiled as she opened the front door.

Otis tipped his hat. "Good day. You must be Katherine?" His sparkling dark eyes told her he wasn't disappointed by her appearance. He formed the words with a rich Southern accent that she discovered to be appealing. She found she wanted him to say her name again and again.

"Yes. And you are Otis." Her voice sounded colorless when compared with his drawl, but he didn't seem to mind.

"Indeed."

"It's lovely to meet you after all these years." She stepped aside for him to enter.

The dog barked. "Yes, yes," Otis said. "You are Miss Katherine's gift, if she will accept you."

Katherine gasped. "For me?"

Otis nodded. "Yes. For you. You wrote to me how much you love animals, and I thought a large farm such as yours would have plenty of room for this little mutt to roam."

"I wouldn't call him little." Katherine got down on her knees and rubbed the dog affectionately. He yapped and licked her cheek. "Or a mutt."

"He likes you."

"And I like him." She smiled and hugged the collie around the neck.

Otis chuckled. "I would agree, now that you mention it. He's but a pup, yet judging from his parents, collies both, he shall grow to a right fine size. I haven't named him yet."

"Oh, we shall think of a name together!"

Mother chose that moment to join them in the parlor. She

stood a few feet behind Katherine. "Good afternoon."

Betsy bounded in behind her, beaming from ear to ear. "A dog!" She rushed to the collie and rubbed his neck. "She's so cute!"

"She's a he," Otis said. "And you must be Betsy."

Remembering her manners, Katherine made the proper introductions.

"Welcome. I am so glad you will be staying with us awhile," Mother said. "Along with your pet."

"Oh, he's not my pet." Otis said. "He is my gift to Katherine."

"I know you won't mind, Mother," Katherine interjected.

"Not at all. We have plenty of room for a dog to roam." Mother smiled.

Betsy patted the dog's fur. He panted and almost seemed to smile at the little girl. "This is the best gift ever!" She beamed at Otis.

"I'm glad you like him." A pleased expression covered Otis's features.

Mother didn't let the dog distract her from her duties as hostess. "I know your trip was long and arduous, Otis. Might I provide you with refreshment?"

"I made a cherry pie yesterday," Katherine added. "I used my own preserves."

"My, but that sounds tempting. I do insist on having a slice, if you would be so kind," Otis said. "But if you ladies don't mind, I'd be much obliged if you would allow me to place my trunk in my quarters so it's not in everyone's way here in the parlor."

"Never you mind about that. Mr. Jones will show you to your room when he comes in from the fields." Mother swept her hand toward the door on the side of the parlor that led to a staircase. "But just so you know, yours is down the hall, first room on the right."

Katherine hurried to open the door for Otis. "That was Ralph's old room. He's off at college."

"He didn't return home for the summer?"

"No, he's taking classes. He wants to graduate a semester early if he can," Katherine said. "He's engaged to be married. Remember how I told you?"

"Oh, yes. I do remember you mentioning that. Well, I promise to take good care of his room in his absence."

"I'm sure you will," Mother said. "Come, Katherine, help me dish up the pie."

"Can I take the dog for a walk?" Betsy asked.

"That's *may* I take the dog for a walk," Mother corrected.

Betsy nodded. "May I take the dog for a walk?"

"That's better. As long as you promise to be careful," Mother admonished.

"I will! What's his name?"

"We haven't decided yet," Katherine said. "Do you have any suggestions?"

Betsy thought for a moment. "Well, he is big and fluffy. Maybe Furry?"

"Furry." Katherine scrunched her nose. "I don't know. Doesn't have much of a ring to it."

Betsy thought again. "Mother said something about him having plenty of room to roam. Maybe Roamer?"

"Roamer. Hmm," Katherine said.

"I think Rover would be better," Mother suggested. "What do you think, Otis?"

"Rover is a fine name for a dog of this nature."

Katherine agreed. "Rover it is, then."

Betsy smiled and headed out the door with Rover.

"I see you've made someone happy," Katherine noted to Otis as she showed him to the parlor.

"I'm glad. But what about you?"

"Oh, yes. Who wouldn't like such an amenable animal?"

Katherine followed her mother into the kitchen. "So how do you like him?" Though she felt confident Otis wasn't within earshot, nevertheless she whispered.

"I think he seems mighty nice. No wonder you corresponded with him so long."

Katherine reached for the metal door of the top shelf of the stove. She often took advantage of this closed compartment just above eye level. It kept food warm and soft, but it wasn't so hot that it cooked food further. Retrieving the pie, she breathed in its fruity, yeasty aroma. "I hope he's not too disappointed in me."

"Whatever would give you such a notion?"

Katherine set her pie on the pine table so her mother could slice it. "I don't know."

"Well, get that idea out of your head. Any man who'd be disappointed in you would be a fool anyhow."

Katherine grinned as they took the pie in to the parlor to serve their guest. They found him sitting on the horsehair sofa. He looked comfortable, as though he belonged there.

Katherine set the tray on the coffee table. "I brewed some tea this morning. I remember you writing me that you like a nice glass of iced tea in the afternoon. I even added a sprig of mint just as you told me you like."

"Thank you. How kind of you to remember my little idiosyncrasies." He took a taste. "Ah! Refreshing."

He seemed to enjoy the sweet treat, complimenting Katherine on her pie. In person he proved as amiable and charming as he had in his letters. She was certain Father would like him, too.

Then again, would he? Perhaps Father wouldn't like Otis at all. Once he was discharged from the navy, Otis had gone back to work in an office. From the looks of him, he had never picked up a hoe or milked a cow. Christopher, on the other hand, felt at ease with anything having to do with farming.

"Do you like to hunt?" she blurted in the middle of his discourse on his aunt's latest trip abroad.

"Hunt?" Otis chuckled and sliced the pie with his fork. "Why would you want to know such a thing? Surely hunting doesn't interest you."

"I must say, Katherine, what did possess you to ask such a question?" Mother asked.

"I. . .uh. . ." Katherine didn't want to admit that she had been thinking about how Christopher loved the outdoors. Hunting was one of his favorite fall and winter activities. "I know how much Father loves to hunt, and I thought maybe the two of you could try it some time."

"In that case, yes, I do hunt from time to time." His eyes twinkled. "Mighty fine pie. Mighty fine." He took another bite.

"Thank you."

Pie consumption notwithstanding, Katherine waited for him to elaborate about his hunting trips, but no details seemed to be forthcoming. Christopher, on the other hand, would have launched into a story about his last hunting experience. She suspected Otis's enthusiasm for the sport was lukewarm at best. She wondered how Father, an avid hunter, would greet such news.

Considering the notion seemed foolish. So what if Father and Christopher shared a love of hunting? There was no requirement that any suitor of hers would have to love the sport even though they did eat game throughout the winter as part of their survival. Still, she supposed in a large city like Charleston, people didn't have to eat game—at least not game they shot themselves—to get through a long, cold winter. What winter there was in Charleston. Otis had written to her about the palm trees and how a body could be comfortable year round in a temperate climate. Why, they hardly had any snow at all down there. Certainly no more than a few flakes.

She visualized a picture of her Maryland farm covered in a blanket of white as revitalizing as a fresh cotton sheet on a hot July night. She couldn't see such an image where palm trees grew.

An unwelcome portrait of the times she and Christopher took sleigh rides in the snow came to mind. She tried to shake these images from her head, but they persisted. There would never be sleigh rides with Otis. Not in the tropics.

Why am I comparing him to Christopher? Otis is charming and gentlemanly in his own right. What is wrong with me? Christopher is a childhood acquaintance. That is all he ever could be.

An alternate voice in her mind argued, *A childhood acquaintance, yes, but then, why can't you get him off your mind?*

Mother's quiet voice interrupted. "I understand Otis is quite a writer."

Katherine forced herself back into the conversation. "Oh, yes. Not only are his letters quite entertaining, as you already know, but of course his poetry is, too." Katherine shot her guest a look. "I hope you don't mind that I have shared some of your verses with Mother and Father."

"No indeed. I am flattered that you think my scribblings are worthy of such notice."

"Maybe you'll decide to write a book one day. One of my other friends—Christopher—wants to write a book." Now why had she said that?

"Christopher. That name sounds familiar." Otis paused in a thoughtful manner, but he didn't seem perturbed. He nodded. "Ah, yes. Weren't you corresponding with him while he was at the university?"

Had she told him that? "Yes. Yes, I was. He's just a child-hood friend."

"I think it's endearing that you've kept in touch all these years."

"That's not so hard," Mother pointed out. "He lives just down the road." She cocked her head eastward toward the Bagleys' farm.

Katherine would have let out a groan if manners had permitted. Why did Mother have to be so helpful? She did her best to recover. "I have always tried to encourage him. He wants to write a history book or an important biography some day."

"Is that so?"

"Yes, and I think he will succeed. He's quite brilliant in all subjects."

"Indeed." For the first time, Otis seemed vexed.

"I—I know you're very smart as well, too, Otis," Katherine added.

"Thank you for that." Otis set his empty plate on the table.

"Might I offer you another slice of pie?" Mother asked.

Otis patted the striped vest that covered his belly. Katherine confirmed her first observation that despite his willowy frame, Otis's abdomen appeared portly for a man under the age of thirty, but she decided extra layers of fat lent him a look of prosperity.

She set her mind back on the query at hand. "Christopher's father needs him on the farm, and he's studied agriculture so they can grow crops more efficiently. But I do hope he will take time to write his book. Maybe in the winter when the work on the farm is less taxing."

"Oh, there's always something to do on a farm. The livestock don't take a break in the winter," Mother said. "They still expect to be fed. And the cows must be milked twice a day, and of course there are always eggs to be gathered."

Otis pondered Mother's observation. "Now that you make mention of such tasks, Mrs. Jones, I must say, farming does sound quite different from a normal business. I suppose I had never given working the land for a living much thought. I don't have it in my blood, as they might say."

Katherine hadn't thought about the idea that her friend harbored no love for farming. Her family had occupied their piece of land for three generations. Her grandfather Jones had granted parcels of acreage to her uncles for their own home sites, and she expected they would further divide up the land so her cousins could live on the same site in peace and comfort.

Katherine had never thought about living anywhere else or adopting any lifestyle other than that of a farm wife. What if Otis really did think he might cart her off to South Carolina? Would she be happy amid palm trees and in sweltering heat most of the year, even if they did decide to live near the Atlantic Ocean where she could wet her feet and enjoy the cooling effects of the water? Katherine had never seen the ocean. She had only seen pictures of it in books. If the photographs were to be believed, the water met the sky in a never-ending mass. She pictured a scene of uninterrupted blue on blue. What would it look like in reality? She shrugged but kept the idea to herself. Living near a vast body of water held no special appeal to her. The idea of seeing the ocean in real life felt akin to traveling to Europe one day. Both offered a distant fantasy that might be tempting but not appealing enough to pursue with determination.

"So what is your favorite chore, Katherine?" Otis asked.

She jerked back into the present. "Chore? Oh, I suppose I don't mind baking. Although it's a bit warm to undertake too much kitchen work at present."

Otis nodded his head toward his empty dessert plate. "You certainly display a knack for baking."

Katherine smiled at his approval. As her mother extolled Katherine's talents in the kitchen, she resumed her daydreams. She had always pictured herself helping her husband—whoever God planned for her—on a farm. She would assist in tending the livestock, making sure the chickens were fed, the cows milked twice a day, and the pigs slopped so that they would fatten nicely for butchering. She could almost smell salted cured ham, aromatic slabs of bacon, and fried fatback.

Her thoughts returned to her imaginary future husband. She would help him plant peas, corn, turnips, potatoes, and strawberries in spring. As she thought, she could almost feel plowed dirt give way beneath her shoes. Disturbed from its rest, the dirt left little particles on her feet in protest. After tending to the gardens throughout the summer, Katherine would help with the harvest. She anticipated spending weeks canning the harvested vegetables and making jelly and preserves—strawberry from the small patch they would keep and grape from a few vines she would maintain of deep purple Concord grapes. Like the Proverbs 31 woman, she would keep her family well fed over the winter months.

At night she would relax by crocheting blankets, mittens, hats, and scarves for her own children and extras for any babies her friends might be expecting that year—just as she was stitching a pair of white booties for the baby Vera's sister Alice expected to arrive soon. She would sew clothes from colorful fabrics she had ordered from the *Wish Book* or saved from patterned flour sacks. When snow covered the ground, she would embroider a fine seam so the family would have fresh linens for the summer. She would bake for Christmas and inhale the scent of a freshly cut cedar tree decorated with strings of popcorn and peppermint candy sticks. Her children would find nice round oranges and walnuts in their Christmas stockings, and each would have a new pair of mittens and socks she fashioned herself.

"My, Katherine, but what are you thinking about?" Mother interrupted.

She startled. "Oh, nothing. Just about crocheting."

"Crocheting? Oh, yes, you must show Otis that blanket you're fashioning." Mother leaned toward him. "It's the most beautiful shade of red. I am trying to convince her to enter it in next year's fair."

"Perhaps she should."

The fair. Was there such a thing in Charleston? She wondered what life in Charleston would be like in comparison. Perhaps she would be expected to patronize a seamstress instead of buying fabric and a sewing pattern from the dry goods store. Maybe a laundress would come to her house to wash her clothes and iron her linens and Otis's shirts. Katherine had to admit that was one chore she wouldn't miss. Standing over a heavy, hot iron while trying to coax wrinkles out of starched cotton wasn't her idea of a fun way to pass an afternoon. Nor were sweeping and dusting, two chores that always seemed to beckon. Maybe having others to help in the city would be a blessing.

But then she thought about how her friend Vera once told her about the rank odors of Baltimore: manure, garbage, too many people crunched together. Katherine stole a glimpse at her beloved front yard, flush with magnolia trees that stood fifty feet high and were covered with waxy, dark green leaves. The back and both side yards were equally majestic and offered a lush array of trees that God Himself had planted before her grandfather's birth. She recalled the sweet, cool, fragrant breezes that descended from their boughs.

Though Otis never wrote in so many words that he planned to court her, she suspected that he wanted to visit her home in Maryland in part to see if she would one day make him a good wife. After all, they had been writing letters to one another for years, and she had not as of yet been spoken for.

She wondered how many trees Charleston could hold in a yard. Few if any, she imagined. Could she make herself content with a window box planted with small flowers, maybe petunias? She wanted to scrunch her nose at the thought.

Light shone through Mother's spotless windows and fresh curtains. Who wanted to smell foul odors all day when the country offered open air and sunshine? Then she remembered how she adored newly picked vegetables and fruits. Vera had once mentioned friends in Baltimore who rented a plot of land so they could have a garden. Imagine! Even then, she couldn't see how a city garden could hold the capacity to produce much of a crop. She speculated that Otis was wealthy enough to purchase a house with a yard that could be called spacious in a city. Yet at the same time, she imagined that on such limited space, she could put up a few jars of jelly at most.

What about meat, milk, and eggs? She'd have to purchase those at a market, she supposed. In any town, raising her own chickens and cows would be out of the question.

She held back a sigh. No wonder city women had garden clubs and society meetings. The city offered nothing for them to do all day!

At that moment a chicken that had ventured closely to the house clucked, a sound she heard through the open parlor window. The clucking seemed to beg her to stay.

What is the matter with me? Why are my thoughts running wild? What has this visit from Otis put in my head?

She knew as soon as the questions entered her mind. His

presence introduced new possibilities for her future. Possibilities she had never considered.

"But of course, though farming is not for me," Otis explained to Mother, "I give farming and farmers my highest respect. Working the land is a noble profession."

"I'm sure that's what Katherine thinks, don't you, Katherine?" Mother prodded.

"Indeed!"

"Is that all you have to say?" Mother chuckled and shook her head. "You'll soon find my Katherine is seldom so silent."

Katherine felt her cheeks flush. "I'm sorry."

"Never you mind," Mother assured Otis. "She'll start talking soon enough."

Katherine resisted the strong urge to turn her gaze up to the ceiling and back, but such a motion would only make her seem to be the little girl her mother portrayed her to be.

"With all due respect, Mrs. Jones, I find Katherine's speech to be quite charming."

Mother sent him an approving smile.

Flattered, Katherine ventured an observation. "One good aspect of farming is that you have a chance to rest a little in the winter, along with the land."

"Hello! Do I hear voices in the parlor?" Father's tenor grew a little louder with each word as he made his way toward them from the kitchen.

"Yes you do, dear," Mother called.

Father crossed through the archway.

"Father!" Katherine rose to her feet. "Otis is here."

She noticed the contrast between Otis's pressed suit and Father's denim overalls. His shirt had started out the day crisp and clean, but now the sleeves were filthy and the collar filled with dust. Out of consideration for Mother, he had wiped the mud from his boots, but the smells of the outdoors hung about him and wafted into the parlor, mixing with the pristine and feminine atmosphere of the formal room.

Otis rose. "Good afternoon, Mr. Jones."

Katherine couldn't help noticing that Otis, on the other hand, could have posed for a gentleman's shaving lotion advertisement in a fine periodical. Not a hair strayed out of place. The part in the middle looked so straight that it could have been the model for a school child's ruler. His deep-hued hair shone, and his fashionable dark mustache had been tamed into place with a liberal application of wax. His white collar held so much starch that there was no danger of it bouncing out of place. Likewise his dark suit could carry him into the finest dining establishment with ease, complemented by shoes that appeared never to have journeyed a mile.

She could only hope that her father would be impressed by Otis's immaculate appearance. He peered at the young man standing by the sofa, but what Katherine saw in his eyes didn't bespeak overwhelming approval. In fact, she couldn't discern by the look on his face what Father thought. She wondered why.

"Oh, yes. The war hero and avid letter writer. Afternoon, Otis." Father took off his hat, spotted with sweat on the brim, and wiped his brow. "We've heard good things about you from our Katherine." He smiled and extended his hand in greeting. Then he looked at his dirty, sweaty palm and decided to wipe it against soiled denim overalls. "Uh, maybe we'd better shake another time."

"I don't mind a little dirt." Nevertheless, Otis withdrew the right hand he had offered. A shadow of relief crossed his face. "I was just remarking to the ladies how I think farming is a noble profession."

"A noble profession." Father seemed to contemplate the notion. "I reckon it is at that. Only I don't feel like I look so noble at the moment." A chuckle escaped his lips.

"That's quite all right, Mr. Jones. Sometimes office work doesn't leave one looking, or feeling, so noble, either." Otis broke out into an affable grin. For that, Katherine felt grateful.

"Why don't you wash up and let me fix you a big piece of cherry pie?" Mother suggested to Father.

"The one Katherine baked?"

"Yes, sir," Katherine answered.

"Sounds good." He winked at his daughter and then exited, intent on his task.

Katherine allowed herself a grin. Food. Sustenance, especially a cherry pie with delightful red fruit filling and a buttery crust, could turn many an acquaintance into a lifelong friend.

Since he had been promised a treat, Father didn't dawdle but returned right away.

"I'm not surprised you baked the pie yourself, Katherine," Otis observed. "Your cooking skills are indeed splendid."

"And that's only the beginning," Father promised. "Katherine will be preparing fried chicken for dinner tomorrow. You'll see then that she can also make a superb cake."

"I'll look forward to that." Otis patted his belly.

"I understand you brought us a collie? Betsy seems quite enamored by him," Father observed.

"Yes, indeed." Otis smiled.

Father nodded, and both men soon were talking about the merits of the breed.

As the afternoon waned, Katherine could see that despite Otis's difference in outlook on life, he was a brother in Christ and showed respect to her parents. By the time five o'clock rolled around and the cows beckoned for their second milking of the day, Father seemed to embrace Otis—if not wholeheartedly, at least as well as could be expected for a man he had met only that afternoon.

Who could ask for more?

four

Later that night, Katherine knelt beside the twin bed, fat with quilts sewn by her mother and her mother's mother. She kept her favorite on top. The red, white, and blue octagons alternated in a pleasing patriotic pattern. Even though early summer weather meant the coverings weren't needed for warmth—demonstrated by a pleasant breeze that blew in through crisp curtains—she liked to keep them on her bed for the familiarity and comfort of home. Never mind that she kicked them off the bed during her sleep and had to straighten them each morning.

Before she shut her eyes so she could concentrate, she glanced at her shelves. Her book collection was sparse but meaningful to her: a copy of the King James Version of the Bible and several well-known novels. On the next shelf down was a collection of display dolls—four in all. Two had been gifts from an aunt as souvenirs from trips. A Cajun doll hailed from faraway New Orleans, and a Betsy Ross doll reminded her of history lessons she learned about Colonial America. The third—a blond Southern belle she named Rosemary and had begged for over the course of several months—had been a Christmas gift. And the last—another Southern belle who could have been Rosemary's sister—she had bought with money she had earned from picking berries and selling them at the market in town one summer. She had named the fourth doll Cherry. She wondered if Otis would mind if she brought her doll collection to South Carolina, or if he would think her babyish for wanting to hold on to mementos of her girlhood. She knew Christopher wouldn't mind. Most likely he could recall the story behind each doll.

Christopher. There he was again, occupying her thoughts.

Closing her eyes and bowing her head, she would remember to thank God for His bountiful provision and for Otis's safe arrival in Maryland. The stiff braided rug was digging into her knees. One day, she would own a soft rug so she could pray in comfort. Or at least, relative comfort. She shifted her position and pondered Otis. As she expected from their lively and lengthy correspondence, he fit right in as though he had been living with them all his life. And there she was, planning to make him think she was accomplished in a number of pursuits. Maybe she shouldn't push her plans forward. Not even for Miranda. Was her idea of friendship misplaced?

❧

The next day Katherine heard a horse clomping up the drive. She pulled back her curtains and was surprised to see Christopher ride up on his gray and black horse, General Lee. To her shock, her heart lurched. What was Christopher's mission?

Just as quickly, her excitement turned to vexation. No doubt he had come to visit Otis, to see what he was like. Why, Christopher even carried a gift. Judging from the shape of the wrapping, the offering was a jar of Mrs. Bagley's famous damson plum preserves!

Like a Ferris wheel going around and around, her emotions for him softened. How nice of him to be so thoughtful.

Thoughtful because he was curious. Hmm.

Wishing to change out of her plain housedress and into something that made her feel more presentable for company, she hurried to her oak wardrobe, which offered six dresses.

She had worn her fashionable yellow one yesterday, so that wouldn't do. A beige Sunday dress complimented her slim frame but was much too showy for everyday.

She regarded the remaining four clean housedresses. The first was the color of a soft pink rose petal. The second would be considered more fashionable, but it had been sewn from a less showy but good sturdy natural cotton. The third and fourth were too heavy for spring wear, so she ignored those and opted for the more fashionable lightweight garment. Slipping into the cream-colored dress in a hurry, she then pulled on her stockings and tied up her boots. With deft fingers she twisted her hair into a chignon. The result was agreeable. Her hair looked like a soft, dark pillow framing her face, with wisps falling attractively along each side. She pinched her cheeks in the right places to heighten the pink color and bit her lower lip a few times. Pleased with the result, she hurried downstairs to greet the men.

They were chatting like old friends before she even set foot across the parlor threshold. Christopher appeared to be relaxed as he swayed back and forth in the rocker. Otis looked nonchalant, poised on the sofa.

Her stomach lurched. Had Christopher already told him about Miranda's plan? But no, Otis looked too congenial to have just experienced disappointment. She sent Christopher a fearful glance, but the look he returned to her indicated no intrigue. So he wouldn't betray her! Or did he hope she would change her mind and go back on her plan? She imagined the second scenario was more to his liking.

At that moment, Otis regarded her with widened eyes and a softened countenance. Apparently he still felt her appearance was agreeable. Christopher's clean-shaven jaw tightened when he eyed Otis watching her. Certainly he wasn't jealous!

Christopher's gaze traveled Katherine's way, and his blue eyes lit with pleasure. His unspoken approval was enough to make her reconsider her plans to fool Otis.

Almost.

After the men rose from their seats and the three exchanged greetings, Katherine took the remaining vacant chair, a blue overstuffed model favored by her father. She felt grateful since its presence meant she didn't have to choose to sit beside Otis as Christopher sat by himself across the room. Still, they were close together since the formal parlor was small.

As the threesome talked about little of consequence, Katherine compared the two men. Otis was a polished gentleman, just as his letters had indicated. But Christopher was both polished and more down-to-earth. While he didn't dress in a manner as formal as Otis did, he still conveyed confidence that seemed to make Otis's expensive and fashionable attire much less important than Otis likely meant for them to be. Christopher put on no affectations, employed no exaggerated mannerisms, and no flattery fell from his lips, but his ways communicated genuineness that Otis somehow seemed lacking.

Wouldn't it be funny if I ended up sending Otis home and was courted by Christopher?

Until that moment, she hadn't thought of Christopher in romantic terms. She wondered how the idea, so remote before, suddenly struck her without warning. She had never thought of him as anything more than a fond friend. So why did she suddenly become aware of his gentle manner and the way he looked at her when he thought she wouldn't notice?

"I read something of interest in your local paper today," Otis ventured late in the conversation. "An evangelist is planning to visit the area."

"A common occurrence this time of year," Christopher pointed out.

"Indeed. So do you plan to go to the revival meetings?" Otis inquired, looking at Katherine.

"Um, I hadn't thought much about it one way or the other. We go to church every Sunday, and we always have a revival for a whole week come summertime."

Otis cleared his throat. "Faithful attendance to one's place of worship is commendable, to be sure. How long has your pastor served your church?"

She thought for a moment. "Ever since I was a little girl. I vaguely remember the first pastor. He retired long ago. Reverend Michaels is the only preacher I truly remember."

"I see. Then I suggest you might find interest in discovering for yourself how another man of the cloth approaches the religious questions of the day." Otis's statement seemed to be a challenge.

"Sure. But I still don't think there's a minister alive who can outpreach Reverend Michaels," Christopher opined.

Otis chuckled. "I'm sure this evangelist won't give Reverend Michaels any competition. But why don't we go to see him all the same?"

"Well, if I weren't willing to engage in adventure, I shouldn't have a houseguest from another state, I suppose. All right, then. Let's go." Her heart increased in its beat as she took a risk. She turned to Christopher. "You'll come along, won't you?"

He looked surprised. "Me? Are you sure?"

"Of course, I'm sure. It wouldn't be the same without you."

"Well, then. Why not?" Christopher smiled.

Katherine felt much too happy that Christopher had accepted. She decided not to ponder what that might mean. At least, not at the moment. She could worry about it later.

"Are we still on for the concert some time during my stay here?" Otis asked, interrupting her musings.

"Concert?"

"Yes." Otis looked at her quizzically. "Surely you won't mind that I make mention of this in front of your friend Christopher, since he is certain to be included in your plans."

"Uh, of course."

"Oh well, perhaps you are not aware, Katherine. Miranda said in her correspondence to me that I must visit Maryland some time—"

"She said that?" No wonder he had decided to make the trip.

"Why, yes." He continued undeterred. "And she said that when I did, all of you would put on a concert. Wouldn't that be splendid?"

"Uh, splendid indeed."

"I certainly hope that event comes about. She suggested that I might add a song or two on the piano. I've been practicing several of my favorite tunes ever since her missive arrived."

"How sweet of you," Katherine noted.

"Yes, how sweet." Christopher didn't sound as sincere. He crossed his arms.

If Otis was bothered by Christopher's aside, he didn't let them know. "Miranda also mentioned that your church will be putting on a talent show later this month. Perhaps the concert among friends will be good practice for that event as well."

"Indeed." Katherine hadn't given the talent show much thought. Now Otis was recruiting her to take part. If he wanted her to participate, she would do so to please him.

"Christopher will be invited to the concert, certainly?" Otis prodded.

"Of course, Christopher will be invited." She looked at him.

"And you will be playing the banjo for us all, won't you?"

"I thought you were talented at the banjo, Katherine," Otis said. "So, Christopher, perhaps the two of you will be playing a duet?"

Katherine wasn't sure why she felt her face flush. "No, Christopher and I haven't had a chance to practice a duet. Although that does sound like a fine idea for another time. No, I plan to play the lap harp."

"Ah, yes. The lap harp," Otis said. "I'm sure you'll sound like an angel."

Christopher chuckled with so much suddenness that he nearly spit. Katherine would have poked him in the ribs had he not been sitting too far away for such a reprimand.

"I fail to see why that is so amusing," Otis remarked.

"I'm sorry. It's just that—that—"

Katherine held her breath, waiting to hear what he might confess.

Christopher looked at Katherine and then back to Otis. "I've known Katherine since we were both little, and I've seen her look less than angelic at times."

"Christopher!" Katherine huffed.

Otis chuckled. "I'm glad to hear you are human. I'm not sure I could live up to the expectations of a true angel."

"I'm sure you could try." She crossed her arms. While Christopher could have revealed her secret, she wasn't sure she was happy with his confession that she was less than perfect even though she was well aware of her flaws. To hear the fact expressed out loud by a friend was disconcerting, somehow. She decided to deflect to another tangent. "But speaking of an angel, Betsy will be tap dancing in the show."

"I can't wait. First, you must tell me, Christopher, about Katherine's not-so-angelic moments," Otis prodded.

"Certainly you don't want to hear some boring old story about my childhood," Katherine protested.

"Oh, a little harmless fun couldn't hurt. I know you have a sense of humor, Katherine," Otis pointed out.

"I have the perfect story!" Christopher launched into one of his favorite accounts about how the class bully dipped her pigtail into an ink well.

"That happened with a girl and boy at my school, too," Otis countered. "Seems children everywhere have the same thoughts."

"Apparently." Christopher chuckled. "But did the girl at your school break her slate over his head?"

Otis thought for a moment. "No, I think she cried and told the teacher."

"Not Katherine. She fought back. Wally had a bruise on his forehead for a week." He laughed.

"Mother wasn't so amused," Katherine pointed out. "She had to cut off three inches of my hair. For the longest time, I felt like a boy." She groaned.

"I'm glad to see your hair grew back. No one could mistake you for a boy now," Otis observed.

She flushed. "Thank you."

As the men shared other amusing childhood anecdotes, Katherine sat in silence. Yes, it was going to be a long visit, indeed.

five

As General Lee trotted down the path, Christopher barely noticed lush trees dressed in the peak of their emerald finery or the scent of the crisp open air with its mixture of fresh plant odors and earthy animal aromas. He was much too pensive to take in familiar, though beloved, surroundings along the road.

The dilemma he faced left him with a sense of unease, and he didn't know what to do about it. He desperately wanted to expose Miranda's misguided plan, not because he desired to be judgmental, but for her own good. What had gotten into Miranda, wanting to put on airs for this acquaintance, a man Katherine knew only through letters? He admired Katherine's desire to protect her friend, but he couldn't condone the deception.

Christopher had known Katherine all her life. And here was this stranger, an interloper, being treated as though he mattered more than anyone else. Christopher pictured Otis leaning back on the divan in a relaxed posture that stated his special standing at the Joneses' place. Christopher found himself glowering at the dirt road. The image of Otis made him want to spit.

In just a day, Otis had settled into the Joneses' house and acted as though he was their social director, religious adviser, and royal guest of honor. Sure, he seemed like a nice fellow on the surface, but anyone could act all high and mighty when no one knew him from Adam.

He wondered what Otis was like at his home in South

Carolina. He said he had a job at an office somewhere in Charleston. He dispensed such a fact with the air of one who served President Roosevelt. Christopher could see that his rival fancied himself important. Well, maybe he was important. Maybe what he did in his office was more important than slopping pigs and milking cows every day.

With the thought, he tightened his grip on the reins.

Christopher could never deny that anyone who wore a suit to an office, which no doubt Otis did, could appear more dashing and handsome than a man in overalls. He looked down at his plain cotton shirt and pants. Since he had dressed with the intention of pleasing Katherine, he had made sure his clothes were clean, but they certainly weren't expensive. Not even store bought. He had donned his best everyday shirt and pants. From his available wardrobe, Christopher couldn't have dressed better. Maybe Otis could get away with sitting around all day in a Sunday suit. He was a stranger, after all. But if Christopher had worn his Sunday suit to see Katherine, she would have thought him peculiar. Possessed of a fever, even.

Christopher tried to shake the image of Otis out of his mind, but he couldn't. He kept remembering how the other man looked as though he was wearing something out of a *Wish Book*. The most expensive suit they manufactured, in fact. And his gold cuff links, octagons with scalloped mother-of-pearl edges, were engraved with three scripted initials bold enough to be seen from across the room.

Christopher sighed. He had scrimped and saved to afford college tuition. Though he looked forward to a bright future, he didn't anticipate a life filled with luxury. His dressy cuff links were unetched, silver-plated ovals that he only wore once a week to worship service. The contrast between the cuff links alone made him see that he could never give Katherine a life in which she could afford to buy luxurious frivolities. Even if he could, where would Katherine go donned in fine silk and crocheted lace every day? Worship service at church and the occasional wedding celebration called for fancy attire, but for the most part, farm wives chose sturdy, serviceable dresses since they engaged themselves in chores for the better part of the day. Delicate fabrics and excessive amounts of lace wouldn't survive long on a woman who toiled in a steaming hot kitchen and smelly chicken coop.

Christopher ducked to avoid a low-hanging tree branch, but his thoughts remained uninterrupted. If Katherine stayed on the farm with him, she would never know days of relative leisure. She deserved a life filled with garden club meetings and with luncheons where the women gossiped and played games and enjoyed indulging in afternoon teas. But if she chose life on the farm, she would have to work. Truly Katherine deserved better than an existence filled with drudgery as Mrs. Christopher Bagley.

Lord, what is Your will? Just a month ago, I was certain You would have blessed my marriage proposal to Katherine. Now she's got another man visiting her and her family, and her mother seems to like him a whole lot. Even Mr. Jones doesn't seem to be immune to Otis's charm and flattery. I admit to the sin of envy, Lord. I wish I could be in Otis's place, to be able to see Katherine any time I like. I long for her, Lord. I wish Your will was for me to marry Katherine. I have wanted that for a long time. But if it isn't, I'll let her go. I promise.

Even as he promised, Christopher felt his stomach tighten as though it had been wrapped in bailing twine. He knew he was being too hard on Otis. If the newcomer hadn't been a serious rival for Katherine's affections, Christopher might even have liked him. He seemed intelligent and nice enough for a city dweller. But he couldn't like Otis. He just couldn't. If this was a test from God, it was one he was failing. Miserably.

Christopher approached the redbrick house he had called home since infancy. Grandpa stood on the front stoop, waving for Christopher to hurry.

"Coming!" he called.

Grandpa nodded and went back into the house.

Christopher studied the low-lying sun on the horizon and realized that supper would be ready soon. He wasn't sure he could eat. But for Mother's sake, he would try.

❧

"Vera, I'm really having second thoughts about this concert," Katherine admitted the next day as they enjoyed a glass of iced tea over the kitchen table at the Sharpes' farm.

"Just tell Miranda."

"Don't you think I've tried? No matter how much I protest, she only makes me feel like I'm not her friend unless I go along with her plan. You should see how she can turn on the tears."

"I can imagine. She can really make you feel like the world's going to end if she doesn't get her way, can't she?"

"Yes, and you know I've never been one to deal with guilt well."

"Neither do I, or maybe I'd have the courage to confront her." Vera sighed.

"Looks like us two sissies have to put up with this plan, then. I really do appreciate your help, Vera. I have to say, I am looking forward to the day Otis goes home."

"What a shame. I take it you two aren't going to be courting, then?"

"He's never said the first word about it. And to tell you the truth," Katherine confessed, "I'm glad. He's nice and all, and he even brought me a dog—"

"A dog?"

"Yes. A beautiful collie. We named him Rover. I must say, Rover has made fast friends with Betsy. She plays with him more than I do."

"No doubt Rover has helped Otis find his way into Betsy's heart, too."

"I think so," Katherine agreed, setting her empty glass on the table. "But she's always been fond of him. He pays attention to her and sends her little trinkets from time to time."

"He'll make a good father one day."

"I'm sure."

"Just not for your future children?" Vera prodded.

Katherine shook her head. "No, not for my future children."

Vera sent her a knowing smile. "Then Christopher must have won after all."

Katherine felt her face redden. She wished she had left a swallow of tea in her glass to cool herself off. "I don't know. . . ."

Vera laughed. "All right. I won't say another word. Besides, we have more immediate concerns. Namely, this issue of the harp."

"I know. I'm sorry Miranda told him that I could play the harp. And I'm even sorrier she talked me into trying to pretend I can."

Vera's sigh reminded Katherine of how her mother sounded when she was a little girl and had forgotten to feed the animals. "So, what song did you order?"

" 'I Send My Heart up to Thee!' That won't be too hard to mimic, will it?"

Vera sent her glance to the ceiling and back. "It won't be easy."

"You'll keep your promise, won't you? You'll teach me how to move along with the notes so it looks like I'm playing? For Miranda's sake?"

"You know, Katherine, I think it would be much easier if you would just learn the song and play it for real."

"Learn the song?" The idea sent chills of uncertainty up her spine. "But what if I make a mistake and hit a sour note? Or even worse, what if I forget the tune altogether and have to come to a grinding halt?"

"So what if you do? Then at least everyone will know you were playing for real. And anyhow," Vera added with such haste that Katherine wondered about her sincerity, "that won't happen."

"I don't know," Katherine said. "In spite of my reluctance to go along with Miranda's suggestion, I still think she had a good idea. I want to make sure the performance is error-free. It's a good thing you can sight-read music so easily."

"For the first time, I wish I couldn't." Vera sighed.

"You do think you can learn it by the time they're expecting me to play, can't you?"

"Yes. I just hope for Miranda's sake—and yours—that no one will realize the sound of the music is coming from the next room." Vera freshened both of their glasses of tea from the pitcher she had kept sitting on the table.

"I think it will be close enough." Without adding more sugar, Katherine took a sip of her freshened beverage.

A terrible thought occurred to Katherine. "Do you think your sister's harp will sound the same as the harp I'll be playing?"

"I doubt anyone will notice. It's not as though we'll have a professor of music among us." Vera scrunched her lips. "Are you sure you want to go through with this?"

"I absolutely do not want to go through with this."

Vera's eyes widened.

"But I must," Katherine assured Vera before she got too

attached to the idea that the plan had changed. "But only for Miranda's sake. I never would have thought up such a scheme myself."

"I doubt you would have. You have a bright mind but not a scheming one. If Miranda had only used her brains for good and not for mischief, we would all be happier."

"True. But Miranda doesn't mean any harm. I know she doesn't. She's just the playful type."

"You're too forgiving."

"Maybe I am. But I'd rather be known as too forgiving than too judgmental."

"So there's no way I can talk you out of this wild idea."

Katherine shook her head.

Vera put up both hands in surrender. "Oh, all right. I can see there's no drumming any sense into that hard head of yours. But I want you to know that the only reason I'm going along with this is because I know the concert will delight Alice and her husband."

"You're a good sister to Alice. And a wonderful friend to me."

"I can only hope my gesture of friendship won't be the ruination of you." Vera pointed her forefinger at Katherine. "You are taking a mighty big chance of making a fool of yourself in front of everybody we care about. I know you have no idea how to play the harp. Does your family even own one?"

"Uh, that's another thing. I was hoping you could loan me yours so I can practice at home. I'll borrow the one in the music closet at church to use that night. I'll only need yours until Otis goes home." She crossed her arms. "I know that fine instrument has been sitting idle ever since you went to Baltimore."

Vera set her gaze toward the parlor even though the harp wasn't visible from the kitchen. "I admit I haven't plucked the first note on it since I got back. Mrs. Alden preferred the pianoforte. For once, I was glad I had suffered through lessons with Mr. Montgomery all those years."

Katherine remembered the stern teacher and concurred with Vera's sentiment. "I imagine Mrs. Alden misses you."

"I'm not so sure. I think she's happy with her new daughter-in-law."

"Well, you have much better things to do than to be a companion for an elderly woman and her grumpy son."

A wry grin crossed Vera's lips. "I imagine Raleigh is much less grumpy now that he's found love."

"Hmm. Maybe so." Katherine realized that Vera had adroitly led her onto another topical terrain. If she didn't recover, she'd leave without the treasured instrument. "So you'll let me take the harp? I promise to take the best care of it in the world."

"Oh, all right. But you must promise to return it as soon as Otis goes home."

"Of course." Katherine rose from her seat and embraced her friend.

❧

"Won't you have another slice of peach preserve pie, Otis?" Looking pleased, Mother sliced her knife through a thick slab of iced dough and cut into the meats of soft fruit baked to a deep orange hue.

Otis patted his stomach. "Oh, I don't know, Mrs. Jones. I already ate one mighty big slice. And your fried chicken and mashed potatoes were simply splendid. I don't believe I've ever tasted such marvelous yeast rolls since the days I was a boy eating Sunday dinner at my dear grandmother's." He looked skyward and lowered his voice to a somber tone. "May the Lord in heaven rest her sweet soul."

Mother straightened her lips into a respectful contour for a moment, then turned the corners of her mouth upward. "So you must have another roll in memory of your grandmother."

"I think I'll take the pie instead." He offered his dessert plate. "Thank you mightily."

Katherine suppressed a smile. Since his arrival, Otis had ingratiated himself to her mother by complimenting her appearance, housekeeping, and cooking. He had made friends with her father by fishing with him and helping tend to the livestock. And he still looked quite stylish and smart while doing so. She had expected him to wear his best clothes at first but to relax later in the visit. Yet to her surprise, Otis didn't seem to own any clothing that wasn't the latest fashion. Even his everyday clothing looked as though it had been sewn by an expert tailor using the finest fabrics. She marveled at his style.

Nevertheless, Katherine could see through Otis's affected appearance and flattery even if her mother could not. She realized he was trying to impress her by gaining her parents' approval. Judging from Mother's eager motion in placing another large slab of pie on his plate, Otis's plan could be labeled a success.

Father didn't smile as he stirred three teaspoons of sugar and a generous stream of cream into a cup of rich black coffee. "Didn't Christopher perform well in church last night?"

"Christopher?" His name slid onto Katherine's lips more easily than she meant. Otis peered at her from the corner of his eye. "Yes. He always sings well. Don't you think so, Otis?" She sent him a smile she knew to be too bright.

"I hadn't heard him sing before last night, but I'll take your word for it."

Katherine twisted her lips. Otis had perfected the art of withholding compliments from Christopher.

"Yes, Christopher always sings for us at the midweek service.

We missed him while he was away studying at college. He's a fine boy," Father added.

Katherine tried not to cringe. She knew this was her father's way of advising her not to make a decision too quickly. She felt heat rise as a flush of embarrassment covered her. She looked at Otis. If Father's observations perturbed him, he didn't show it. Perhaps his preoccupation with flattering Mother covered his vexation.

Relieved that Father's remark hadn't started an unfortunate strain of discussion, Katherine picked at her sliver of pie and occupied her mind with other thoughts.

❧

Immediately after Sunday school, Katherine rose from her seat. Miranda had been eyeing her all through the lesson, and Katherine wanted to make her escape before her friend could snag her. No doubt Miranda wanted to involve her in yet another scheme to fool Otis. Katherine's plan almost worked, but Miranda caught up to her before Katherine could avoid her without being rude.

"How is it going with Otis?" The man in question had carried a discussion on a minute theological point past the class hour and, just out of earshot, was making a brilliant argument before a rapt circle of their peers.

Miranda ogled him dreamily. "He certainly is dashing, isn't he?"

Katherine glanced at him. "I suppose, in his way."

"And smart." She stole another glance at the former sailor, then turned back to Katherine. "You don't seem impressed."

Katherine deliberately kept her eyes from focusing on Otis and held her voice to a near whisper. She motioned for Miranda to join her in walking to the sanctuary. "He's nice enough. He even brought me a beautiful collie."

Miranda took in a breath and kept pace. "He did? How marvelous."

"Yes, he is a gentleman. But. . ." Katherine didn't want to tell Miranda that her war hero couldn't hold a candle to Christopher.

"But what?"

"Never mind. What did you need to tell me?"

"How did it go with the harp?"

"Vera agreed to help."

"I knew she'd come through." A mischievous light glowed in Miranda's eyes and just as quickly dissipated. "But now we have another problem. Remember, he thinks you're an expert horsewoman."

"Oh, no. I forgot all about that." Katherine groaned. She looked her friend in the eye. "Miranda, this has gotten out of hand. I think we have to put a stop to it and confess all to Otis."

"No! Please don't!" She ground her heel in the floor.

"Then what am I to do?" Katherine peered at the front of the sanctuary and noticed that Otis had moved away from their friends and now occupied himself by conversing with her parents since they had already taken their seats in a pew. Christopher, donned in a rich blue robe, had already positioned himself on the third row of the choir loft.

"That's what I wanted to talk to you about. I have a plan."

Katherine clutched her Bible. "I'm afraid to ask."

"Don't worry. My idea is brilliant. If I may say so, you and I could be mistaken for sisters from a distance. So I have a simple plan. Next Thursday, when are your parents sure to be in the house—or at least nowhere near the stables?"

Katherine thought. "A little before lunch, I suppose."

"Good. I'd like to come to the barns then. If you could dress in your riding habit, I'll do the same, and we'll look very much alike. At that point, all I have to do is take Ash out and jump a few hurdles. After that, I'll disappear into the barn. Then you come out, pretending you're the one who performed the jumps."

"I don't know. I don't think I like such an idea."

"Oh, please? For me? I promise you I'll never ask another thing of you in my entire life!"

Katherine sent her a reluctant nod and then hurried to sit beside Otis in the pew. Miranda strode to her place in the front row of the choir loft. They had just seated themselves when the pianist struck the first note of "Amazing Grace."

Katherine tried to concentrate on the sermon and sing with focus, but her mind was elsewhere during most of the service. As the benediction was said, she resolved to make amends by paying full attention the next week and at the Wednesday evening prayer service.

To Katherine's surprise, after worship Christopher caught up with her on their way out of church.

She stopped by an aromatic rose bush near one of the front stained-glass windows and eyed his Sunday suit. Though not as fine as Otis's, the cut flattered his muscular, trim, and tall form. "You slipped out of your choir robe fast enough."

"I hurried on purpose, I must confess. I have to talk to you."

Katherine looked toward the dispersing crowd of women dressed in colorful Sunday dresses and men in their best suits. Her parents were still lingering with a few of the other congregants. From all appearances, Otis didn't mind chatting with one of the engaged women from their Sunday school class. Katherine wouldn't be missed, at least not for a few moments. She turned her full attention to Christopher. "All right. What is it?"

His stare brooked no room for play. "I saw you talking to Miranda."

"So? Miranda's my friend."

"I know you both too well. Katherine, I wish you wouldn't go through with her ridiculous plan."

"I know it seems ridiculous to you, and maybe it is. But haven't you ever done anything ridiculous for a friend?"

Christopher thought for a moment. "Maybe when I was a boy but not recently. No doubt, I'm not as sentimental as you are about your friends."

"Perhaps not."

"Being a loyal friend is an admirable quality." He smiled and touched her arm briefly. The unexpected contact sent a pleasant shiver though her. "I just don't want to see you suffer for your sacrifice in giving in to Miranda's misguided plans."

"Miranda doesn't mean any harm. I'm sure all will be well."

"I wouldn't be so quick to caution you if I thought following through with her scheme would be good for all concerned. But in my view, the whole idea is pointless. As much as it pains me to say it, anyone can see that Otis fits right in with you and your relations. I don't care what Miranda says. I don't think you have to prove anything to him."

"Maybe you're right, but I promised Miranda I'd go along with her. And even if I have to suffer a little, I wouldn't be a good Christian witness if I went back on my word." Her resolve wasn't inwardly as strong as she made herself appear, but she didn't want Christopher to see her waver. With a deliberate turn, she set her gaze toward her family and felt thankful when Mother motioned for her to join them. "I've got to go. See you soon." She rushed toward Mother and relative safety.

❧

Christopher watched Katherine depart. He wanted to hasten to her, to make her see reason, but he remained frozen in place.

He was left so irritated by the exchange that he couldn't bring himself to move. During church, he had been even more vexed to see Katherine sitting by Otis. No matter what Christopher did, it seemed he couldn't win.

Grandpa tapped him on the shoulder. "There you are, boy. We've been looking for you."

"Sorry, Grandpa. I had to talk to Katherine."

Grandpa rubbed his chin, touching a bit of gray stubble that he had missed in his efforts to shave that morning. "Yep, that Katherine girl is a mighty fine young woman. Too bad she's let herself get carried away by that Otis feller. He's a fancy dresser, all right. Too fancy. Anybody can see he don't belong in these parts."

"That's what I've been thinking."

"Yep. I been watchin' him. He talks a fine streak. Flatters every woman around. Every man too, for that matter. Even had some kind words for me this morning. But I don't know. He seems just a little too slick. Yep, a little too slick. He reminds me of Homer James. He almost got ahold of your grandma, you know. But she saw through him. With a little nudge from me." When Grandpa winked, Christopher noticed that the sharp blue color of his eyes hadn't diminished since Christopher was a boy.

"But how can I help Katherine see?"

Grandpa watched the Joneses and Otis board their buggy. "I don't reckon I know right off the top of my head, Son. But the good Lord in His wisdom will show you how. Just you watch."

"Watching is pretty hard, Grandpa."

"Sure it is. Just be careful you don't watch too long or hard, lest you wait too long to take whatever action needs takin'."

"I'll try not to." Still, as Christopher and Grandpa walked

toward the Bagleys' buggy, another thought occurred to the younger man. An even worse thought.

What if the tricks end up leading Katherine straight into Otis's waiting arms?

six

Your *Wish Book* order arrived!" Mother's voice, traveling from the kitchen to Katherine's room early that morning, carried a mixture of anticipation and curiosity.

Katherine set her boar bristle hairbrush on her oak vanity and rushed down to the kitchen. Since she hadn't taken time to secure her hair into a chignon, loose locks flew outward as she hurried. She couldn't let Otis see her open the box or even let him see the package. What if he guessed she had ordered sheet music? And what if he asked her to play the song for him, then and there? He was the persistent type, just liable to make such a request. If he did, he'd find out all too quickly that she couldn't play a note on the harp.

How she wished she had the courage to tell Miranda they had to call the whole thing off! She remembered the times she had tried, to no avail. Miranda would only succeed in crying and making her feel terrible.

"That's a mighty flat box," Mother noted as Katherine reached for it.

She nodded and departed before Mother could stop her or ask questions.

As soon as she returned to her bedroom, she unwrapped the package. The paper smelled crisp and new. The sweet smell of fresh ink greeted her nostrils. She studied the picture on the cover. A beautiful blond woman was pictured, with cheeks as red as apples and a subdued-looking mouth that appeared ready to burst into song. Katherine opened the music and stared at the notes.

"Hmm. Not too much of a challenge. At least not for someone as experienced at the harp as Vera. I'll bet if I go over to the house now, she'd play it for me." Since she'd completed her before-breakfast chores, Katherine knew she could slip out for a few moments without too much chastisement from Mother.

Turning to the round vanity mirror, she looked at her reflection and deemed the results of her toilette acceptable. With a quick motion, she pinned her chignon into place and set off down the steps to leave for her friend's house.

"Good morning, Katherine." Otis had already sat down at the table, waiting for Mother to serve him a helping of scrambled eggs and bacon.

"Good morning, Otis. And a fine day it is, too. If you'll be so kind as to excuse me, I have an errand to run. I must see Vera."

Mother lifted her spoon and shook it at Katherine. "At this hour?"

"She's an early bird. No doubt she rose hours ago," Katherine assured as she bounded through the back door.

"But Katherine, you must have a bit of breakfast."

"I will, later. I promise." Katherine rushed to set her bicycle upright, placed the sheet music in the basket, and headed off for Vera's.

On the way, her growling stomach objected to the fact that she had left without a bit of her mother's scrambled eggs. But her task was too important to allow her to stop for sustenance.

The aroma of spicy pork sausage cooking on the stove tempted her palate as she skipped up the stairs to the kitchen of the Sharpes' farm.

Vera's slackened jaw and widened eyes revealed her surprise.

"Uh, good morning, Katherine. You're making the rounds mighty early."

Alice scooped up a sausage patty as she and Katherine exchanged pleasantries. Expectant motherhood agreed with Alice, who was an older version of fair-haired Vera.

Vera nodded toward the package Katherine held. "What have you got there?"

"The sheet music, silly. Just like I told you."

Vera didn't crack a smile. "Oh. Well, maybe we can take a look at it after breakfast. Will you have some sausage and eggs?"

Katherine sat down at the table. "Why, how kind of you. You know, I am a bit hungry, so I do believe I will accept your offer."

As they ate and chatted, Katherine hardly tasted the sausage and eggs. After the meal, Katherine asked Vera if she would play the song.

"My, but judging from your excitement, this must be the most exciting song ever," Alice observed. "Mind if I listen with you?"

"Of course not," Katherine said.

Vera escorted them into the parlor, where the lap harp awaited. Vera studied the music for a moment, nodded her head, and began to play.

Though Alice hadn't been informed about the significance of the sheet music, Katherine listened in anticipation. As expected, the song was delightful. When Vera finished playing, Katherine clapped. "Oh, Vera, that's beautiful!"

"Indeed it is," Alice agreed. "Won't you play it again?"

"Of course." Vera gave Katherine a knowing look. "Katherine, why don't you go into the kitchen and fetch me a glass of water? If you would, please."

Katherine wondered about her friend's sudden thirst and then realized what she meant. She wanted Katherine to hear how the music would sound coming from another room, since that was their plan.

"Vera, can't you wait for a glass of water? Honestly!" Alice protested.

"I don't mind, Alice," Katherine assured her all too quickly. "Might I fetch you a glass as well?"

"No, I'm fine, thank you." Alice settled into her seat and rubbed her expanded abdomen.

As Katherine poured Vera's water in the kitchen, her excitement over the music drifting in from the parlor vanished. Vera had been right. There was no way the music would sound immediate enough to fool their audience. If only she had listened! Exhaling in defeat, she steadied her emotions and re-entered the parlor with a glass of cold water and a smile.

"That was just as beautiful the second time," Katherine told Vera.

"Indeed, yes," Alice agreed. "What a lovely song, Katherine. I can see why you're excited about it and wanted to share it with Vera. Certainly you plan to learn it yourself."

"Yes. If Vera will teach me." Hearing the lack of enthusiasm in her own voice, Katherine realized her zeal for Miranda's plan had long since abated. The depth of the web of deception Miranda had woven was materializing. Yet rather than the clever spider awaiting a reward for a well-spun snare, she felt like the foolish fly. Silken words felt like threads of barbed wire, encasing her in a trap from which no desirable means of escape offered itself.

"Just be sure you do." Alice smiled. "I'll leave you girls to your visit. Sewing awaits me. Don't dawdle too long, Vera. The eggs need to be gathered."

"Yes, Alice."

Oblivious to Katherine's inner turmoil and Vera's part in the plan, Alice exited the parlor, humming the tune.

"Oh, Vera, you were right. My idea will never fool anyone. What am I going to do?" Katherine wailed.

"Just what I told you that you should have done all along. Learn the song."

"But I don't have time."

"Of course you do. If you work at it."

"Will you help?"

Vera handed her the sheet music. "Do I have a choice?"

≈

"After all this time here, I can't believe I have yet to hear you pluck the first note on the harp," Otis observed.

Katherine peered at the ground long enough to show Otis she had no intention of responding. Otis, Katherine, Vera, and Christopher had formed a group, making their way to their respective buggies. They had just passed a delightful evening among their favorite crowd, hosted by the parents of their mutual friend Lily.

"Oh, believe it," Christopher muttered.

Katherine poked him in the ribs and gave him a warning look from the corner of her eye. So far Christopher had been a true friend. He hadn't betrayed her, even though she'd been nervous all night that he might say something to Otis to make him suspect that Katherine wasn't all that Miranda had portrayed her to be in her letters. But Christopher hadn't so much as hinted that anything was amiss.

Not that he was a big talker in any event. He'd been quiet all night. Katherine saw him observing Otis from time to time, but Christopher never challenged Otis on any of his opinions, even though some of his ideas were citified or poorly supported, at least to Katherine's way of thinking. Katherine knew Christopher hadn't changed so much since he went away to school and had now returned to make a life for himself on his family's land. Perhaps Christopher didn't say a great deal because Otis wouldn't be here long. Or maybe because Christopher didn't like Otis much. He never mentioned it, and Otis had never wronged Christopher, but she sensed that Christopher was wary of him.

"So how much longer are you going to keep me in suspense about your talent as a harpist?" Otis asked.

"Not too much longer, I hope. I want to be sure I have a special song prepared for you. I've been practicing with Vera." There. She had stuck as closely as she could to the truth. That should help. "Isn't that right, Vera?"

"Yes, that's right." Even Vera couldn't deny the truth of that statement.

Katherine sent her a grateful look. Regret at following Miranda's schemes was starting to take its toll. She wanted to please Miranda and Otis, too. Yet the burden had become wearisome.

"Are you sure you can't play something for me in the meantime? I don't mind if I have to hear a sour note or two as you practice." Otis stopped beside the Joneses' buggy.

"Or three or four," Christopher chided.

"Christopher!" Katherine admonished him.

"I'm sorry. You'll have to pardon me, Otis. I've known Katherine so long I forget sometimes she's all grown up and I shouldn't tease her."

"As long as Katherine doesn't mind, I suppose." Otis sounded grumpy. Then, as though remembering where he was, he composed his expression into a grin. "My, but you have a nice church." He observed the landscape. "And such nice countryside here. I'm tempted to extend my stay."

"You're certainly welcome to do so," Katherine blurted.

He smiled. "So which one of your many talents will you be displaying for the talent show next week, Katherine?"

Katherine stiffened. She had been so busy worrying about the harp and her lack of expertise in horsemanship that she had forgotten all about the talent show. Well, she didn't forget, really. Not entirely. But she didn't think of herself as one of the contestants. And now Otis had made it clear that he expected her to take part. At least Christopher and Vera were in on the ruse so they wouldn't blurt out something embarrassing. Still, she wasn't sure how to answer.

"Why don't you try all of them?" Christopher winked.

Katherine shuddered. How could he suggest such a notion? Didn't he know Miranda's reputation was at stake? Certainly she couldn't be expected to betray her friend. Poor Miranda would be devastated if Katherine went back on her word.

If only she could go back in time and convince Miranda that trying to deceive Otis wasn't a good idea. Then she recalled how Miranda had cried and carried on to the point that Katherine felt helpless to deny her. Even if she could turn back the clock, she would make the same decision to help her friend. A decision that was looking less wise with each passing moment.

Otis chuckled. "If she did, the show would last all night, and she'd be the only contestant!"

"At least you'd win, Katherine," Vera noted.

Katherine nodded. Otis meant his observation as a compliment, but she hardly felt flattered. Instead, guilt crushed her soul. She cut her glance to Christopher. He looked pensive. She swallowed, glad to arrive at their buggy. While she wanted to climb in, the others looked at her, awaiting an answer. "Uh. . .I. . .uh. . .I hadn't thought much about entering the talent show. I thought I'd just watch."

"What?" Otis protested. "And deny everyone the pleasure of seeing you perform? I won't hear of it."

"I'm sure it's too late. Mrs. Watkins must have everyone lined up by now."

"No, it's not too late," Christopher assured her. "In fact, they'll take entrants up to the last minute."

She kept from shooting him a mean look. "I don't know. . . ."

"Then it's settled," Otis said. "You'll enter." He snapped his fingers. "I have a splendid idea. Why don't you dance a fine ballet number for the show, and I'll play the piano for you? I'm sure if I put my best foot forward I can learn a number before then. And certainly you can as well."

A mixture of gratitude, surprise, and guilt shot through Katherine. "You'd do that? You'd play the piano for me?"

He bowed. "I'd be honored."

Katherine wished he weren't such a gentleman. "Otis, I have a confession to make."

As soon as the words left her mouth, she could sense a spark of electricity between Vera, Christopher, and herself. She felt her face turn several shades of hot red. "Speaking of the ballet, I'm afraid I'm out of practice. I wouldn't dream of dancing in front of the whole church."

He looked disappointed. Katherine glanced at Vera and Christopher and saw disappointment on their faces as well. How had she managed to let everyone down in one fell swoop?

Otis recovered first. "Oh. Well, I can't expect you to keep all of your skills up to their best level at all times, and I'm sure the church members would concur. But never fear. You still have many talents to offer the show. And I can still help. I know a musical number calling for the banjo, harmonica, and piano. Perhaps we could perform a duet. You could play the harmonica and banjo as you indicated, and I can accompany you on the piano."

Katherine could see that Miranda had dug a deep hole for her, and she was teetering over the edge, about to fall into the abyss. Learning a few ballet moves surely would have been easier than mastering not one but two instruments. She had to think quickly. "That is indeed a splendid notion, Otis. And once again, I appreciate your willingness to accompany me. That is so sweet and kind of you." She thought she heard Christopher emit a small snort. "But I have a better idea. Why don't we instead provide background music for Christopher to sing a solo?"

"Oh, yes indeed!" Vera chimed in. "Katherine, I think this is one of the best ideas you've had in a long while. What do you say, Christopher?" She turned to Christopher, eyes shining. "Why don't you enter the show and perform with Katherine and Otis?"

It was Christopher's turn to hesitate. "But I hadn't planned to enter the talent show."

Assuming that since Vera supported the idea, she would help her, Katherine thought it politic to add, "As you pointed out earlier, there is practically no deadline. You can enter moments before the show starts. Oh, you must enter, Christopher." She tapped Vera on the shoulder. "Why don't you play along with us? I think we might even win!"

"Maybe I shall," Vera agreed. "Katherine's right. With this pool of talent, we may win!"

"Win indeed." Otis observed.

"Since I have a chorus of insistence, I see that I shall not escape your begging and pleading until I agree to perform."

Christopher's voice betrayed a mixture of regret and anticipation.

Otis spoke up. "I feel I must point out that banjo music hardly works with a piano and a harp. Perhaps a simpler solution would be for me to teach you a piano duet, Katherine. Since you are competent on the harp, harmonica, and banjo, surely one song on the piano would be an easy accomplishment for you." He turned to Vera. "And you can still accompany us on the harp."

"Oh, of course. Katherine is a marvelous pianist," Vera said. "What do you say to Otis's idea, Katherine?"

"I don't know about 'easy,' but I think I can manage." Katherine held back a relieved sigh. Striking a few piano keys had to be less taxing than managing the banjo and harmonica simultaneously. She sent him her sweetest smile. "All right. I'll do it."

seven

In spite of his best efforts not to express vexation, Christopher slammed the door on the way into the kitchen after he arrived home. Instead of his usual crisp voice, Grandpa's words sounded muddled.

He eyed his grandfather, sitting at the table and swallowing. "Sneaking a piece of pie?"

"Don't tell your mother. She's been trying to get me to cut back on desserts, but I won't stand for it. I've lived this long without watching what I eat too close. I reckon the good Lord will see fit to let me live a few more years. And if He doesn't, then I figure I'll be with your grandma sooner than I thought."

Grandpa shuffled to the sink pump and rinsed the dish, washing away evidence of apple pie crumbs. He turned to his grandson. "But you. Well, you're young and another matter altogether. So why are you so angry?"

Christopher tried to think of a way to avoid admitting the truth. "Who says I'm angry?"

Grandpa wiped the plate with the dry dish towel and slid it into its proper place in the kitchen cabinet. "Look here, young man. I've known you since you were nothin' but a little red thing squallin' at the top of your lungs. I know when you're mad. Besides, I slammed a door or two in my day myself." He winked. "So does this have something to do with that sweet little Katherine and the competition from South Carolina she imported for you?"

"Competition? He's no competition for me."

"That bad, huh? Well, I know a thing or two about women. They haven't changed all that much since I was a young buck. You've just got to get in there and show her what's best for her, that's all." He shuffled to his seat, plopped down, and situated himself in comfort.

Christopher took a nearby chair. "And just how will I do that when I'll be singing along with his piano playing?"

"Say what?" Grandpa twisted his index finger in his ear.

Christopher wasn't sure whether to laugh or get even madder. He decided to take the middle road and keep his unwelcome emotions in check. "I got roped into performing with him at the talent show." He relayed the rest of the story.

Grandpa thought for a moment. "Well, I'd normally observe that a situation like that would put him in a superior position. He could be tempted to flub-de-dub on the piano so you would stumble in your singing."

"Oh." Uneasiness visited Christopher's stomach. Such a thought hadn't occurred to him.

Grandpa lifted his forefinger to get Christopher's attention. "But he won't do that. Not with Katherine playing along with him. So I think you came out on top after all, my boy."

Grandpa's encouraging words gave Christopher pause to consider what other good could come out of the situation. "At least Otis won't have Katherine all to himself."

"True. Except when he is teaching her the piano duet."

"Oh, yes. I hadn't thought of that." Christopher's depression returned.

Grandpa winked. "But there's not a thing in the world to stop you from being at every possible practice. So what if that means you might have to hurry through your chores. Skip supper, even. But maybe if she has to feed you, she'll feel sorry for you and pay you more mind. That mothering instinct comes out real quick. It worked with your grandma."

Christopher laughed. "That's what you always say."

"And you can believe it."

"I don't know how much mothering Katherine wants to do. I'm thinking I would have been better off if I had agreed to go along with her plan of deception."

"Now wait just a minute here. It's not Katherine's plan of deception but Miranda's. She's the one who's keeping the pressure on Katherine to make her keep on going along with this silly game."

"You're right. Katherine is not a deceiver at heart. And she never will be. She's too good for that. Too kindhearted for her own good. Every time she tries to wiggle out of the ruse, Miranda cries. She makes Katherine feel really bad. It makes me mad just to think about it."

"What do you think made Miranda decide to tell all those stories, anyway?"

Christopher thought for a moment. "I don't know, but I have a feeling Miranda never thought Otis would make the journey all this way to see us. She thought she'd never get caught, I suppose."

"I've seen Miranda in action. Now she doesn't think I'm looking. She thinks I'm too old to notice or to be noticed. Maybe she's got a point there."

"Grandpa, that's not so."

The older man held up his hand. "Don't you go arguing with me, son. I'm just saying that people say things in front of me they wouldn't dare utter in front of their parents. And I've seen that Miranda friend of yours brag within an inch of her life. Gets carried away, she does. I suppose she can't help it. Don't know why she feels she has to brag so much, though. She's a right pretty girl. Well off, too, judging from all the jewelry she likes to wear all the time. Guess she just wants attention. But to drag poor Katherine into it, that's just wrong."

"I know. And I wish she hadn't," Christopher said.

"Well, she's trying to do a good turn for a friend, and I suppose I can't fault her so much for that. But as for you, two wrongs don't make a right. You're doing the right thing not to be a part of a scheme. They'll all learn. But I have a feeling they will have to learn the hard way."

"As much as I don't like this Otis guy. . ."

"Yep, I never much cared for competition either. He seems nice. Too nice."

"That's just it. I can't find anything wrong with him. He's charming. And there he is, right in her house. She doesn't stand a chance." Christopher sighed. "Maybe they should be together. Maybe I'm the one interfering in God's plan."

"I doubt it. Just be sure to be around when she falls. You only have a short time left before he has to go back to where he came from. Those days will pass much sooner than you think."

Christopher remembered Otis's hint that he'd like to remain in Maryland longer. "I don't know. I'm afraid he's taken such a liking to Katherine that he wants to extend his visit. What's wrong with that man? He told Katherine he had a business to tend to. But I don't see how he'll get anything done playing around here forever. Doesn't he ever do a lick of work in his sorry life? Of course," Christopher ranted, "he's using the excuse of the church people and the appeal of the country-side as reasons to stay longer, but I can see right through him. The snake." He cut his glance to his older relative, who had always been his mentor. "Can you take a guess, Grandpa?"

He shrugged. "Maybe he's independently wealthy."

"Maybe so." Christopher remembered the expensive-looking

suit he wore to the gathering that night. "He certainly dresses in clothes that look like they were store bought. And not from just any store but a fancy city tailor."

"Yes, I have to admit, Otis cuts a fine figure. But you look better than he ever could even when you've got on dungarees with pig slop all over 'em. Of course you do. You take after your old grandpa." He wagged his forefinger. "Not that your mother was any slouch in her day, either. Don't tell your father I said so, but she had quite a few offers before he came along and stole her heart." Grandpa rocked his chair back on its hind legs. "But your daddy has made her happy, and they gave me and your grandma you and your brothers and your sister. I'll always be grateful to him for that." He nodded. "Yep, one day I hope you can look back on your life with as much satisfaction as I have in mine."

"I'm not sure I will if Katherine decides to abandon me for Otis."

"Maybe you should speak up now before she sets her mind for good."

"Why bother? I can't compete with Otis."

"With that kind of attitude, you never will win at anything." Grandpa's frankness caused Christopher's heart to skip a beat. "Unless all she wants is money. And you won't be giving her a whole lot of that out here on the farm."

"Maybe not, but she'll always have plenty of fresh air and enough to eat. Besides, Katherine isn't like that. Money never interested her. Sure, I know she wants enough so she won't have to worry, but she never seems to care about fine things like some other women. Like Rosette Sims, for one."

"The flirty little brunette who likes to wear her dresses a little lower than she should on top and a mite too short on the bottom?"

"Grandpa! I didn't think you'd notice such things."

"I might be old, but my vision's still good."

"As a matter of fact, she did come to mind. She always wears the most elaborate hats and too much jewelry for all occasions. Even more so than Miranda."

"I see you've noticed her too, then." Grandpa chuckled.

"I don't mean to be prideful, but Rosette has sent interested glances my way more than once." Christopher cleared his throat. "I've never paid her any mind."

He knew why. He was still too much in love with Katherine.

❧

The evening of the harp solo arrived. Vera had planned the small gathering of friends as a way to entertain her sister who was still in her confinement, so she had asked the guests to bring dishes to share as well.

As Katherine crossed the threshold of the Sharpes' kitchen, lap harp in hand, she couldn't remember a time when she had felt more nervous. Well, maybe during the play in her senior year of high school, when she blanked out on her lines and had to ad lib, thereby adding new meaning to the word *comical*. Too bad the skit had been written as a drama.

"Are you ready, Katherine?" Vera greeted her. "You certainly look splendid enough to perform at a real theater!"

"Thanks." She looked down at her dress. "So do you."

Vera blushed. "Hardly. But thanks for the compliment."

Otis entered behind Katherine, carrying a load of food. "Good evening, Miss Vera."

She sent him a pleasant smile. "Good evening, Otis."

"Pardon me for getting right to the point, but I confess this load is a bit heavy. Where shall I put all this food?"

"Over on the table in the dining room, if you'd be so kind. I'll arrange it later." She pointed to a table where other guests had already placed many succulent dishes.

"I'm surprised you couldn't follow the aromas, Otis," Katherine chided. "Everything smells so delicious, Vera. You must have prepared your famous chicken casserole."

"Indeed I did."

"And everything does smell scrumptious," Otis agreed.

As he hurried to comply with Vera's instructions, Katherine whispered to her friend, "I wish I felt as confident as you say I look."

"You have no reason to fear."

Katherine wasn't so sure, and the anxiety in her voice betrayed her sentiments. "What will happen if I falter? I'll look like a fool in front of Otis and Christopher. . . ." She shook the thought from her head.

"I wouldn't worry if I were you. Most people don't know enough about playing the harp to realize any mistakes."

"I don't know."

"You have learned your song well. We certainly practiced enough!" Vera looked toward the door. "Besides, judging from the looks of what Otis brought in, you outdid yourself on the quantity of food. No doubt quality as well."

"I hope so. I cooked all day. Cherry pie, nutmeg cake, vegetable salad, potato salad, even fried chicken. Otis did a lot of taste testing, and he approved all the dishes."

"I can't wait to try everything. Come, let's go greet the others."

Katherine nodded. She managed to relax as she talked to her old friends and got caught up with their lives. Though life moved slowly on the farm and proved predictable, she still enjoyed hearing about each person's joys and mourned with each sorrow. She tried to make her way over to Christopher, but he spent most of the evening with the men, most likely talking about the latest market numbers and other details of running a farm. Though she found the talk fascinating, the men considered numbers and such more their domain, so she tried to look as though she wasn't paying them much mind.

She caught Christopher's eye once or twice, and he looked congenial enough, but he never did manage to finagle his way near enough to her to share a thought or two. Funny, she had missed him while he was away at school, but his chatty letters always kept her informed, so she didn't think much about his expected absence at gatherings. Now that he was always in the same room, she realized how much her fondness for him had grown over the years. Too bad he considered her nothing more than a childhood friend.

Where did that thought come from?

"Why, Katherine," Miranda noted, "if I didn't know better, I'd think you were blushing."

"You must really like Otis a lot," Lily observed.

"He is nice enough." Katherine didn't want to be ebullient about her guest. Otherwise, her friends might get the wrong idea. On the other hand, she didn't want to be too harsh. Why invent a failing just to show them that her heart refused to flutter when he entered the room?

"Maybe you'll be moving to South Carolina before you know it," Lily speculated.

"Now, now, let's not jump to conclusions," Katherine said. "I have no thought in my mind of making any such decision. Otis and I have become acquainted through the exchange of letters. That is all, and that is all I think it ever shall be."

"He hasn't hinted at more?" Miranda's eyes were wide.

Katherine shrugged. For the first time, she wished Otis had flirted with her. Then she would have a story to share amid blushes and shy whispers. But as it was, she did not.

She swallowed. "As I said, he is a kind houseguest. He will be returning to his home soon."

"I see." When Miranda turned her head to eye Otis, her pearl earrings dangled in stride. She fanned herself with a much higher degree of energy than the weather required.

Even Katherine had to admit he cut a fine figure in his tailored clothes.

"He is quite stylish," Lily noted. "But he has nothing on my Wilbur." She sent her fiancé a smile that caught his attention. He smiled back.

Katherine held back a chuckle. Only Lily would say that Wilbur appeared superior to Otis. She looked over at Christopher. He held his own against every man in the room. Every man she knew, for that matter. Even Otis.

"Well." Vera approached from the kitchen and looked at the overburdened table. "It looks like everyone is here. I say it's high time we ate."

Alice's husband offered grace, and they began.

Katherine wasn't worried about dinner. She knew she could hold her own in cooking. For once, she felt relaxed and took time to relish the feeling as she sampled the dishes her friends had brought.

"This cherry pie is mighty good," Christopher remarked later over dessert. "I'm told you made it?"

"Yes, I did. I'm glad you like it."

"I sure do." He grinned. "Your cooking certainly has improved since your teen years. I remember when you brought rock-hard biscuits to a church potluck dinner."

She groaned. "Did you have to remind me?" Still, she cherished his memories. Christopher's observation only brought to light the history they shared, something she never could have with Otis.

Seeming to sense her thoughts, Otis interjected from his perch on the other side of the divan, "Yes, this pie is wonderful, Katherine. I don't remember a time I've tasted better. And Christopher, you must try the nutmeg cake, too. It's absolutely splendid. I had the privilege of being with Katherine as she cooked, so I have already sampled every foodstuff she made. I can assure you, each dish is absolutely exquisite."

"I'm sure." Christopher didn't look too happy.

"What amazes me, Miranda, is that you never told me about this particular skill. Frankly, I think cooking well is much more useful than being able to sing and dance. Much more practical, certainly."

"Katherine is talented in a number of areas, as Miranda told you," Christopher said. "Katherine is much too modest to boast about her skills and talents. Then again, I've known her a long time, and I am well aware of her many gifts."

"Thank you," Katherine said softly. Christopher's kind words meant so much more than any flattery from Otis could have.

Dinner passed all too quickly. Wariness returned later as Katherine went before her friends. Since they were show-offs, the friends played and sang for each other to rousing applause. Miranda took the opportunity to sing an opera tune that impressed all, even Katherine. Upon the song's completion, Otis clapped the loudest. Miranda curtsied several times to resounding applause.

"I know you brought that harp for a reason," Christopher said to Katherine. "Let's hear you play."

"I agree!" Otis said. "She's been practicing with Vera, and I haven't heard her pluck the first note myself.

Katherine swallowed but obeyed their prodding and took her place in front of them.

Father in heaven, I know I don't deserve Thy mercy, but I ask for Thee to stay with me as I perform tonight.

Once Katherine hit the first few notes, she remembered the rest of the song with ease. She even forgot she had an audience of almost everyone in the world she cared about, and as she plucked, she enjoyed listening to the music she created. She almost couldn't believe it when the end of the piece was greeted by unstinting applause and smiles from her friends. She felt pleased and relieved. Vera had been right after all. Learning the song was much more rewarding than pretending to learn it. And her conscience was clear.

Father in heaven, I thank Thee for seeing me through.

eight

After the concert, the group relaxed, seated around the room, and talked among themselves. Otis broke off with Christopher and approached Katherine as Vera excused herself to chat with Miranda.

Katherine gave him a look that she knew expressed her nervousness. She wasn't sure what to expect.

To her surprise and delight, he offered a smile. "You played superbly, Katherine. Even better than I anticipated. And I assure you, that's saying quite a lot."

Katherine smiled, feeling genuine delight in a performance well executed. As Vera had foretold, the effort had been worth the reward. "Thank you."

Otis rose from his seat. "If you'll excuse me, I must say a few words to Miranda. Surely she is to be congratulated for her superb rendition as well. She certainly chose a challenging aria and delivered it flawlessly. Why, she could pass for someone trained in such arts."

"Yes." The fact she felt no jealousy surprised Katherine.

"Is she?"

"Is she what?" Katherine shot a glimpse Miranda's way.

"Why, trained in the art of opera, of course."

"Oh." Katherine tried to recall. "I believe she took lessons some years back. A voice teacher traveled from town to town, giving lessons every week or so. I didn't take advantage of the opportunity, I'm sorry to say."

"That is not to be regretted. Your talents are many." He

nodded once. "Now to congratulate Miranda."

Katherine wasn't alone for long, for Christopher soon walked up beside her. "For once I concur with Otis. Your talents are indeed many. I must say, your performance just now was splendid."

Katherine noticed that Christopher's congratulations sounded heartier than Otis's had. His words seemed to convey that he was happy that she had finally learned to play the harp after years of wishing she could. "Yes. Learning that song—really learning to play it—taught me a lot. I have to give Vera credit for being patient enough to teach me."

"Yes, Vera is a good friend to you."

She nodded and looked over at Otis. He was engaged in animated conversation with Miranda.

Christopher's gaze followed hers. "Otis seems to have made a new friend here."

"Yes."

His dark eyebrows shot up, drawing her attention not only to his surprise but also to his clear blue eyes. "You don't seem to be bothered by his apparent interest in your friend."

"Should I be? I've always maintained that Otis and I are just correspondents. Nothing more."

Christopher didn't seem to mind her admission and changed the topic. Yet she hardly heard what he said as she recalled the trickery regarding the horsemanship that Miranda had planned over her protests. Katherine had decided to make one last attempt to call it off. "Excuse me, Christopher. I have something to say to Otis and Miranda."

"Oh?" His mouth straightened. "You don't want to hear about how Reddy got out of the pen and scared Mr. Crawford half to death?"

"Again?" She shook her head. "That bull has never been one

to be controlled, has he? How many times has he gotten out of that pen?" Nevertheless, she drew out her lace fan and cooled herself with it as she stood in place, a sign of her willingness to listen to his tale of mock woe.

Christopher laughed and finished his story, embellishing the details and making much of the fact that his neighbor Homer, known to be equal parts bully and coward, fell face down in the mud while trying to escape the ranting beast, hurting only his pride but leaving a splotch of wet dirt on his dungarees. Though glad for the amusing interlude, Katherine excused herself from Christopher as quickly as she could when he was done.

She made her way through the gathering, weaving through couples as well as clusters of friends chattering about the latest news. When Katherine reached the couple, Miranda was throwing her head back in mirth. Her earrings dangled with the motion.

"Oh, do let me in on the joke. I always like a good laugh," Katherine said.

Otis's response didn't convey the deference to which Katherine had become accustomed. "Perhaps I should wait until we arrive at your home. I would be remiss if I allowed Miss Miranda to listen to my story again. I never like to bore anyone."

"Oh, you could never bore me, Otis," Miranda insisted. "Do retell the whole story from start to finish. And don't you think of leaving out a single detail on my account."

"Are you sure you'd like to hear me tell my tale again?" Otis asked.

"Indeed."

"All right then. If you will not take no for an answer." Otis grinned and then related a story about his office that didn't seem all that amusing to Katherine, but Miranda laughed again as though she had heard it for the first time.

Katherine wished she hadn't insisted on hearing the story. She took her cue from Miranda and chuckled at the right times. Encouraged by their attention, Otis relayed yet another event, one mildly amusing to Katherine but apparently of great interest to Miranda.

"You are aware that Katherine is an expert horsewoman, are you not, Otis?" Miranda asked when the subject of Miranda's success in horse shows was broached.

Good! An opportunity!

"About that—" Katherine said.

"Yes, indeed," Otis interjected, lifting his forefinger as though he were a college professor about to make a point that would be included on the examination, "You made that quite plain in your letters, Miranda."

"Oh, but I could never compete with Miranda. And I wouldn't want to." Katherine sent a flattering look Miranda's way.

Miranda fanned herself with enough gusto to cause her overloaded charm bracelet to clink with fury. She batted her heavy eyelashes at Otis. "Well, I do have my share of ribbons and praise for my skill. Katherine has complimented me many a time."

"Coming from another expert horsewoman, that must mean a lot," Otis said.

"About that expert horsewoman business," Katherine managed, "I must admit, I'm not quite as skilled as you may have been led to believe. In fact—"

Otis swatted his hand at her and looked at her as though she were a child speaking out of turn. "Our Katherine is the modest one, isn't she?" Otis asked Miranda. "I can see why she's so popular."

"I prefer to say that I am blessed with many friends who

are kind to me beyond what I deserve," Katherine said. "Take Miranda here—"

"Yes, Miranda does seem as though she would make quite a good friend," Otis observed, sending a pleasant smile Miranda's way. "Perhaps you should come along and watch Katherine as she demonstrates her skill to me some time. I was thinking of asking her if we could meet tomorrow, perhaps."

"Tomorrow would work well."

"Good. By all accounts you would appreciate the chance to watch since you will know how hard she works to hone her equestrian skills."

Miranda didn't miss a beat. "I'd love to be there. I'll see what I can do. As you know, I'm always up for an adventure." She sent Katherine a sly smile that Katherine was sure escaped Otis's notice. "Seeing Katherine and her horse would be quite impressive, but now that I recall my schedule for tomorrow, I regret that my entire afternoon is engaged." Miranda let out a larger-than-life sigh. "I'm afraid I shall miss seeing her. Another time, perhaps." The sweet countenance she conveyed to Katherine left no hint that Miranda had any other intention.

Katherine suppressed a groan. Try as she might to confess, an admission wasn't going to take place. Not with Otis and Miranda dominating the conversation as they were. To speak now would only serve to embarrass Miranda. The thought of her friend's tears and recriminations left Katherine with a sorrowful feeling. To reveal all would embarrass Miranda and cause her to break her promise. Katherine couldn't find it in her heart to do either. Any courage she had mustered to speak the truth evaporated. "Excuse me, but I think I'll have another glass of punch."

"Where are my manners? I should have noticed your cup was running low and pardoned myself so I could freshen it for you. Please forgive my breach of courtesy." Otis reached for her cup.

"Not at all." Katherine noticed that Miranda's cup and Otis's were half full. She was tempted to deny him, but he took the cup, leaving her alone with Miranda. Katherine saw an opportunity too good not to pursue. She cleared her throat and started speaking so quickly that her words almost ran into each other. "Miranda, maybe we should call off the whole plan regarding the horse tricks."

Miranda's eyes widened as she shushed Katherine. "Don't speak so loudly. Someone will overhear."

"That wouldn't be such a disaster, I'm beginning to think." She pursed her lips and looked at the tips of her shoes. "I really think we should call it off."

"No. Please. I don't want to lose face in front of Otis. Not now."

A thought flashed through Katherine's mind. "You like him, don't you? You really like him."

Miranda blushed. "He can see me ride—as myself—another time."

Otis returned with two full cups of punch. "I beg your pardon, ladies, but the line for the punch was unbelievable for such a small gathering. Mrs. Sharpe let the bowl run dry and had to replenish the supply. I do believe the entire assembly ran out of punch at the same time." He handed Katherine her cup. "But the wait does mean that I can offer you a beverage freshly prepared."

"Thank you. That is splendid." Miranda said.

"Yes," Katherine said as she accepted her cup. "Splendid."

"As for the wait, never worry for a moment, Otis," Miranda hastened to assure him. "Katherine and I were sharing entertaining confidences, were we not, Katherine?"

"Um, yes. Confidences indeed."

Otis chuckled and took a sip of his drink. "Ah, the whisperings of the fairer sex. Intrigue we men shall never be privy to nor understand."

"Indeed you shall not!" Miranda teased. "For we women need to maintain a few mysteries to keep ourselves interesting to you men, do we not?"

"I'm not so certain. I would venture a guess that you would remain interesting to us, mysteries or no."

As Miranda giggled, Katherine felt her eyebrows rise. Did she ascertain something in Otis's tone that revealed he held a mystery as well? She wondered.

૪

"I'm here!" Miranda called out the next day, catching Katherine at the stables as planned. Seeming to be oblivious to the drizzle that had fallen on and off throughout the day, she flashed Katherine a winning smile. She dismounted from her dapple-gray mare and swept her hand over her red cropped riding jacket and form-fitting riding pants. "How do I look?"

"Great." Katherine looked down at her own outfit, which mirrored her friend's. "We look almost identical," she had to admit.

Katherine looked back toward the lake and saw Otis approaching, carrying a wooden bucket. He'd been fishing with Father for the better part of the day. No doubt she would hear many stories about his successful trip.

Miranda hissed, "That's him! If I don't hide, Katherine, he'll see us dressed alike and know something is amiss!"

Panic seized Katherine. She watched Miranda head into the barn. The plan was set to commence.

Katherine turned toward her visitor and put on her most cheerful face. "Hello, Otis!"

He quickened his pace, approaching her with increasing speed. When he drew close enough to speak to her without raising his voice, Katherine noticed the dank smell of muddy water, wet grass, and fish. He seemed not to notice that outdoor aromas clung to him, a fact that Katherine found amusing in the usually immaculate Otis.

"I came here as soon as your father and I ran out of bait and called it a day. We had an excellent day. I caught an exceedingly large trout that should feed the whole family for one meal at least." He extracted the fish from the bucket and showed it to her.

Katherine concentrated her thoughts on how the fried fish would taste, its flaky meat tender and buttery. "That sounds wonderful. I can fry it up for you tonight."

"Good." He held up the fish for his own inspection and studied it, a boastful look upon his countenance. "I'll dress this fellow here as soon as I see you jump. I don't want to tarry, though, as it wouldn't be fair for me to leave your father with all the work to do. He's at the house now, dressing his catch." Otis, much to Katherine's relief, returned his own catch of the day to the wooden bucket.

She nodded and ducked into the barn. Miranda saw Katherine enter and delayed leaving long enough to make Otis think Katherine had mounted the horse. Then she trotted out in style.

Katherine watched as Miranda and Ash jumped the practice hurdles, one right after the other, in a fluid motion. Still hidden in the barn, Katherine gasped in awe. If only she could make her horse jump in such a way!

Katherine had relaxed until they approached the last hurdle. She watched as the horse slipped. Miranda pulled on the reins, but her efforts proved futile. She lost her hold, fell off the horse, and landed on her side on the ground.

Katherine didn't think about what could happen as she sprinted toward Miranda. No matter how embarrassed she would be, no matter how much pride she would have to throw aside, she didn't care. She had to make sure her friend was all right.

From the corner of her eye, Katherine noticed that Ash had stumbled but recovered. Well-trained and faithful animal that she was, the horse stood beside the hurdle and whinnied, watching what would become of her mistress.

Otis ran to Miranda in the meantime. "Katherine!" he called, obviously not realizing the deception at first. Raw fear made itself evident on his face. He really did care about her! Her heart soared, then plunged.

Reaching Miranda first, he knelt beside her, although she had already recovered and was sitting upright on the ground. He looked into her face. "Miranda?" He paused. "Miranda! What is the meaning of this?"

nine

Katherine could hear the anger in Otis's voice. Guilt shot through her. If he was angry, he had every right to be. The ruse had been exposed, and Otis was about to discover that he had been duped.

All she could do was try to make amends.

Katherine bounded to their sides. "I can explain."

Otis stood and helped Miranda rise to her feet. He pointed to Miranda, and then to Katherine. "You. . .you two are dressed alike. Why? What's going on here?"

Otis's glare stole Katherine's courage. "I'll explain later. We need to tend to Miranda now." She took her friend's hand. "Miranda? How are you?"

Miranda nodded before a wry grin bent her lips. "I've felt better, but I'll be fine."

"Are you in any pain?"

"No."

"That's a relief." Katherine exhaled. "You're standing, and that's a good sign. Try to move your arms and neck. Can you?"

Miranda lifted her arms and rotated them back and forth. To show how well she had recovered, she danced a triumphant little jig. Katherine clasped her hands to her chest. "Praise the Lord!"

Christopher and Vera approached, scaring Katherine since, too absorbed in Miranda's plight, she hadn't seen or heard them. "Mrs. Jones said ya'll were out here. What's going on?"

Otis's face darkened. "What's going on? What's going on?

I have been deceived, that's what's going on."

Christopher shot Katherine a look that conveyed both chastisement and fear.

"It's all my fault, really," Miranda rushed to elaborate. "I took a little fall. Nothing unusual in this business. Everything's fine now. Please don't concern yourself with me."

Christopher's eyes filled with compassion. "I'm so sorry, Miranda. Is there anything I can do to help you?"

"You can help me recover my pride, I suppose. If that's possible." Miranda laughed, a sure sign she had returned to her ebullient self.

Christopher nodded. "Good. But perhaps we should postpone our talent show practice to another day. Apparently none of us is in any state to practice our musical number at present."

"Oh, Christopher!" Katherine said. "I'm so sorry. I forgot all about our practice today. And Vera, I apologize to you, too. Look, we can find some way—"

"Never mind, Katherine." She looked as though she felt sorry for her friend.

Otis glared at Christopher. "You act as though you know what happened here."

"No, Christopher and Vera had no part of this," Katherine explained.

"Be that as it may," Otis said in a controlled voice, "I am very vexed with you, Katherine. I may not be the sharpest pencil in the box, but I can see what's going on here. You and Miranda dressed alike, and you let her use her skill to make me think it was you who was jumping hurdles. Is that right?"

Katherine looked down at the ground. "I'm afraid so."

"It's all my fault, Otis."

Katherine breathed a sigh of relief. Finally, Miranda was

ready to confess, and Katherine was free.

Otis turned to Miranda. "Your fault?"

"Yes. I wrote all those things about Katherine, knowing she wasn't as skilled as I claimed. I never thought you'd visit, but when you did, I panicked. I thought up this whole plan, and I begged her to go along with me in the ruse. She tried and tried and tried to get me to change my mind, to come clean, to confess everything right away, but I was the one who resisted." Tears rolled down her cheeks. She sniffled.

"There, there, now." Otis patted her on the shoulder.

Miranda nodded and took a handkerchief from her jacket pocket. "I—I was too prideful and didn't want to be embarrassed. I didn't want you to know I had lied. I'm so sorry."

"I see that you are," Otis cooed.

Miranda looked up at him with tear-drenched eyes. "Can. . . can you ever forgive me?"

"Of course I can."

"And can you forgive me?" Katherine interjected. "Like Miranda said, I didn't want to be a part of this. I was only going along with it for Miranda's sake, and I'm sorry I didn't have the fortitude to stand my ground."

"What she says is true. Katherine was being a friend to me," Miranda agreed.

"In that case, yes, I can forgive you, too, Katherine." Otis turned back to Miranda. "I can't believe you both went to all this trouble just to impress me."

"To impress you? I suppose you could look at it that way, yes," Miranda said.

"But you shouldn't have risked your life, my dear," Otis said.

"I did no such thing. The hurdles were easy ones. I admit I was surprised when Ash faltered." She looked down at the ground and pointed. "That's the culprit."

They all observed a patch of mud.

Christopher studied it. "That's enough to throw anyone." He threw Katherine a comforting look and touched her on the shoulder briefly but drew his hand back before anyone else noticed.

"The mud was concealed by grass," Miranda said. "I know because I didn't see it myself, and if I had, I would have led the horse around it and not attempted that last hurdle. No one could have predicted that Ash would falter. And it's not as though I have never fallen. The only thing that's hurt on my account is my vanity." She chuckled.

"Perhaps, but I must say, despite your good intention, I am quite upset by this development. I never meant to cause anyone to tell a lie. That distresses me greatly. Perhaps since I have proven to be such a negative influence, I should pack my bags and leave."

"Leave?" Katherine asked. "Otis, I know this has all come as a shock to you, but please do not resort to hyperbole."

"I'm not so sure I am. I will have to think about what my next course of action will be. Maybe I should take the train out on Monday morning."

"But what about the talent show? Will you stay for that? Please?" Miranda implored.

Otis set his heels firmly in the ground. "I don't know if I can be convinced."

"At least watch us rehearse," Katherine suggested, hoping he might change his mind.

Otis withdrew his pocket watch and looked at the time. "It's only two o'clock. I should have time to get to the train station to purchase my ticket if I leave right away."

"Two?" Christopher questioned him, withdrawing his own watch. "I'm afraid your timepiece is not accurate, Otis. My watch says it's already quarter to three, and I have mine set by the jeweler according to railroad time."

"Then your watch should certainly be accurate." Otis harrumphed. "I did notice my watch seemed to act in a sluggish manner before I departed South Carolina. Apparently its performance has not improved since then." He set the hands to the proper time.

"Then it's settled. You don't have time to do anything about your return trip today. You may as well stay for the rehearsal," Katherine pointed out.

"All right, then." He didn't seem too upset that his plans to leave had been derailed. Katherine had a feeling his suggestion had been more bluster than intent.

"Good!" Miranda took him by the arm, a development that seemed to please Otis.

The group walked back to the house in silence. Katherine became immersed in her thoughts. Even though the incident with Miranda had tarnished her relationship with Otis, Katherine was glad they had committed to participating together in the talent show. That meant she could be close to Christopher when they practiced for their performance.

The afternoon had told many a tale. At the pivotal moment of despair, Christopher, not Otis, chose to comfort her. In that instant, Katherine realized that she had ignored a treasure living right next door. She knew she could love Christopher as more than a friend. But after her mistakes, could he ever return her feelings? If he couldn't, she knew she would be getting what she deserved. She had done wrong out of a desire to please a friend.

Now she could see beyond any doubt that what her friend had asked of her was wrong. She never should have let herself get involved in Miranda's schemes. In her heart, Katherine knew that Miranda hadn't acted to embarrass Katherine intentionally.

In fact, Miranda had the highest stake in making sure the ruse was a success. But in hindsight, Katherine discerned that she shouldn't have let Miranda define their friendship. She should have stood up for herself and insisted they come clean about Miranda's letters to Otis. She had learned so many lessons during Otis's visit: the limits of friendship, the importance of courage, and where her heart lay in regard to Christopher.

Then fear struck.

Heavenly Father, has my misguided attempt to help Miranda caused me to lose Christopher forever?

Otis left them to join Father in dressing the catch. As Vera, Miranda, Christopher, and Katherine crossed the porch, Katherine suppressed her disturbing thoughts. Nothing would be gained if the practice for the talent show proved to be a similar disappointment because she was distracted.

Mother regarded them as they entered the kitchen where she was in the process of rolling smooth, creamy dough for dinner rolls. Katherine took in a deliberate breath, inhaling the appealing scent of fresh yeast that filled the kitchen.

"My, but we have quite a crowd here," Mother observed. "How is everyone?"

Christopher answered first, followed by the others' exchange of pleasantries. Mother offered glasses of refreshing mint tea and cups of coffee. As they relaxed for a few moments in camaraderie, Katherine felt eternal gratitude that no one mentioned the mishap with the horse. Nervousness seared her throat as Otis entered, but he busied himself with a quick cleanup at the washbasin and then excused himself to his room. She had the distinct feeling that since he had made no mention of the mishap at that moment, he planned to let it pass. She breathed a sigh of relief. At least he had shown her a small portion of mercy.

"Is everyone ready for practice?" Otis asked after he had taken a brief interlude to freshen himself. Katherine couldn't help but notice combed hair, clean clothes, and the aroma of spicy shaving lotion, no doubt applied to impress Miranda.

She cut her glance to Christopher. He still looked unsullied in a crisp white shirt and blue and white seersucker pants. Vera's encounter with the outdoors left her equally unspoiled, appearing in white and yellow as she did. Even Miranda, dirtied as she was from her fall, beamed so brightly no one would notice how much mud her pants had accumulated.

"I'm more than ready to begin," Katherine offered. "Mother, would you care to watch us perform?"

"I wish I could, but I'm too busy with this dough at the moment. Do play loudly enough so I can hear, will you?"

"Of course." She managed a smile.

As they rehearsed their numbers in the parlor, Katherine noticed that Otis's mood improved. He played with more gusto than usual. She found the development to be no surprise. Miranda provided them with an enthusiastic audience, clapping in resounding approval whether or not they had missed notes. Every once in a while, Mother called out encouragement from the kitchen.

Betsy bounded in from playing outdoors, with Rover following closely. "I heard the music. It sounds so pretty!"

"Thank you," Otis said.

Mother appeared. "Do I hear that dog scampering around in here?"

"Sorry, Mother," Betsy answered and shooed the dog outside.

"Betsy," Mother warned, "you know Rover can't be here in the parlor. Please try to do better."

"I will." She shut the door behind Rover.

"That dog has taken up the worst habit of coming in the house," Katherine said.

"He does that because he loves me," Betsy informed her. "He wants to be where I am."

"That's all well and good, but as far as I'm concerned, he belongs outdoors," Mother reminded her.

"I know. I'll do my best to keep him outside." Betsy scampered to where Miranda sat and took a place beside her. She fingered Miranda's charm bracelet. "Did you get the charm from Egypt yet?"

"Not yet." Miranda smiled. "I am hoping Aunt Tilly can find one in the shape of a pyramid, but of course such a trinket might not be available."

"I hope she finds one. I know it will be pretty if she does."

"Speaking of pretty, what are you going to do for the talent show?"

"Tap dance."

"Oh, that sounds nice."

"Mother is going to play for me." Betsy turned a sunny expression to Otis. "Are you ready to play in the talent show?"

"I'm not sure. I may not be here."

Betsy's chin nearly hit her chest. "Why not?"

"This is news to me, too, Otis," Mother pointed out.

"Oh, please stay, Otis!" Betsy implored.

"I think you should, especially now that I've heard you play. You're so wonderful with music!" Miranda added. "I just don't know what we would do without you in the talent show. Why, I told everyone at church how talented I know you to be, and they're all eager to hear you perform."

"Is that so?" Otis's chest puffed.

"That's so." Miranda batted her eyelashes in his direction. "Oh, please say you'll stay."

Otis paused, much to Katherine's amusement. He was playing up his act for all it was worth.

"Please?" Miranda and Betsy asked in unison.

"Oh, all right." Otis smiled.

"Yay!" Betsy clapped her hands. "So will you play another song for me?"

Since Miranda never professed to Otis that Katherine could play the piano, Katherine had nothing to prove. She felt as relaxed as she could considering that, as she practiced her song, she still felt Otis's eyes watching her. As they continued, she missed a few easy notes and soon realized she wasn't up to form, but they made progress on the musical number. After a half hour, she felt satisfied that they had accomplished as much as could be expected for one day.

"Why don't we call it a day on this music?" Katherine ventured.

"So soon? I was enjoying the show," Miranda objected, though not with vigor.

"Perhaps you will see your way clear to watching us rehearse tomorrow," Otis suggested.

"That is a thought." Miranda smiled. "You've done very well. If I may be so bold, I'm wondering if you might like to take a break and let me entertain you with a song."

"Absolutely!" Otis said. "Will you allow me to accompany you on the piano?"

"That would be my pleasure."

"Your request? Perhaps 'Hello, My Baby.'"

"That's a popular song, indeed, but hardly one that suits my voice."

"What was I thinking? Of course that wouldn't be a suitable tune for your feminine voice."

"Do you know 'Havanaise' from the first act of *Carmen?*"

"You have certainly named a challenging song," Vera observed.

"Indeed it is, and I'm not sure I can do Miranda justice with my accompaniment, but I shall try," Otis said.

Miranda took in a breath and executed the difficult operatic number without a flaw. Such was her skill that even Mother stopped her work long enough to enter the room to hear Miranda sing. When she completed the number, the resulting applause from everyone in the room was genuine.

"I think we could give the others some competition at the talent show," Otis said.

"I think we could." Miranda giggled, then composed herself. "Present company excluded, of course."

Otis glanced at the others. "Of course."

Somehow, he didn't sound convincing.

❧

Horses' hooves pounded against Maryland dirt as the Bagleys' buggy journeyed to the Sharpes' farm after rehearsal.

"Christopher Bagley, you certainly are not very good company today." Sitting in the seat beside him, Vera poked him in the ribs.

"Ouch!"

"Sorry. I don't know my own strength."

"Sure you don't." Christopher rubbed the place in his side where Vera's elbow had prodded. "Another one of those and I won't be able to sing."

"As if you can concentrate with Katherine around."

"I'll only permit you to say such a thing since you are like a sister to me, Vera."

"I'm so glad that's what you think. Someone has to tell you to wake up and hear the rooster crow."

He glanced at the unsightly curves of the horses' rumps,

their hindquarters moving back and forth in rhythm, and the trees that lined the path. Anything to keep from facing Vera—and the truth she was bound to reveal.

"I know what you were thinking," Vera continued, undeterred. "You were thinking that Otis was too much competition for you. Well, if you can't see after the way he treated her today that he is totally and completely out of the picture, then you need a good whack between the eyes with a frying pan."

"And you think you're just the one to do it?" Christopher teased as they turned into the drive.

"Someone has to!"

"Maybe you should tell Katherine what you just told me and see what she has to say about it." As soon as he uttered the dare, he regretted his words. What if Vera called his bluff and really did tell Katherine? What then? He cleared his throat. "Uh, if you have a right mind to. But I think she'd laugh in your face."

"Cry with relief is more like it. I know she's sorry she pulled all those stunts just to protect Miranda."

Christopher brought the buggy to a stop in front of the Sharpe house.

"It's a shame Miranda planned such a scheme." Vera's feet hit the ground, and she let go of Christopher's hand after he assisted her in disembarking. "Truly a crying shame. Katherine really is talented."

"I wish she had said something to Otis right off the bat, though, instead of waiting," Christopher said.

"We both tried to encourage Miranda to be honest once we found out what happened," Vera said. "But you should have seen her let loose with the tears. She put on quite a performance to keep us both involved in her plan."

Christopher nodded. "Knowing Miranda's penchant for drama, I don't doubt it a bit."

"I think Katherine has learned her lesson about the limits of friendship. I know I have."

ten

Four days later, Katherine peered through her kitchen window. She watched Vera dismount from her bicycle and lay it on the ground near the porch. "Is it time for rehearsal again?" They had been practicing often over the past few days. Katherine enjoyed the time she spent near Christopher, but she never admitted that fact to anyone. Not even Vera.

Mother dried a drinking glass. "Yes, it must be. I thought you said they'd be over directly after lunch. They're right on time."

Betsy entered. "Mother, may I go to the general store and buy some candy?"

"I don't know." Mother eyed her. "I had no idea you had so much extra money. Aren't you saving up for Christmas?"

"Yes, but I have two extra pennies I can spare. Please?"

"Well, you've done a good job with your chores lately. I suppose you can go, but take Rover with you."

Betsy smiled and ran out the door, almost running into Vera.

Sheet music in hand, Vera rushed into the house. "Hello, Mrs. Jones."

"Hello, Vera. Nice to see you again." Mother set the glass in the proper place in the cabinet.

Vera nodded, and Katherine noticed her breath came in shallow and fast spurts. "Katherine. Are the others here yet?"

"Not yet."

"At least we don't have to worry about Otis, since he's right here."

Katherine shook her head. "No, he isn't."

Vera's nose wrinkled. "Whatever do you mean?"

"I haven't seen Otis all morning. He didn't have lunch with us. How about you, Mother? He tells you everything. Have you seen him lately?"

"I haven't, as a matter of fact. You know, he doesn't talk much to me anymore." Mother eyed Vera. "I declare, it looks to me like there's been some sort of spat, but Katherine won't tell me a thing for love or money. Now, you wouldn't happen to know about any unfortunate event that might have transpired, would you, Vera?"

"Oh, dear, Mrs. Jones, you are putting me in quite a pickle."

"That's what I thought." Mother rubbed her dish towel in a vigorous circular motion against a defenseless plate. "Hopefully one day she'll see fit to confide in me."

"If I hadn't had a spat with him before, I'd certainly have a right to now," Katherine noted, handing her mother a newly washed plate. "You'd think since he is staying right here with us that he could be on time for practice. But I suppose not."

"If his lack of punctuality at the past two rehearsals are any indication of his dedication to our cause, he may not show up at all," Vera opined. "I wonder why? He seemed so enthusiastic about performing in the talent show before."

"I think I can guess. I have a feeling he's practicing a number for the talent show with Miranda," Katherine noted.

"Really?" Mother nearly dropped her plate. "I admit they made a wonderful team the other day when he played the piano and she sang such a lovely opera number. But what about you? Does he plan to leave you out in the cold?"

"No, I think he plans to be part of our act," Katherine answered. "I just believe he thinks he's so good he doesn't need to practice." Having completed her task, she squeezed water out of the dishrag. "And we have all noticed how he's been absent from the house lately."

"He did go fishing with your father yesterday, so of course we didn't see him much," Mother reminded her.

"Yes, he has developed quite a fondness for fishing, I must admit," Katherine said.

Mother placed a spoon in the drawer. "And that's to our advantage, too. I've enjoyed eating fish more often since he's taken up the hobby."

"I'm not surprised to hear you take up for him, Mother. He does love to flatter you." Katherine untied her apron.

"Katherine! You are being mighty hard on poor Otis."

Father chose that moment to return from his errand at the general store. "What's this about poor Otis?"

"We were discussing his unexplained absences from the house lately," Mother informed him.

Father set down his sack of goods and gave Mother a quick kiss on the cheek. "Yes, I've noticed that, too. Didn't want to make mention of it, though. Wonder what's gotten into that boy?"

Katherine gave Father her rapt attention. She could tell by his voice inflection that he had some idea. But to her disappointment, he only took a seat at the table and made no further effort to reveal his notion to them.

Vera cleared her throat. "I hate to be the one to tell you this, Katherine, but Lily said he's been at the Hendersons a lot lately."

"The Hendersons?" Mother asked. "Whatever is the attraction there?"

"So I was right after all." Father chuckled. "I believe her name is Miranda."

"Well, of all things! To think he'd abandon our beautiful Katherine for the likes of Miranda Henderson!"

Katherine tossed her apron on the peg fashioned just for that purpose. "Oh, he didn't abandon me, Mother. He and I were never more than acquaintances who enjoyed a vigorous exchange of letters."

"But I thought his real intention of visiting us here was a desire to court you," Mother protested.

"Maybe it was, at first. And maybe I thought a little bit about the idea myself, just in passing, mind you. But long ago, I decided I didn't want to take things further with him."

"Really?" Father prodded.

"Really. I have no desire to live so far away. If I moved to South Carolina, I'd hardly ever see you at all. And Otis doesn't live on a beautiful farm. I don't know that I'd like living in a city like Charleston so much. Why, Hagerstown is too big for me."

"You do have a point," Mother said. "I don't want you to move, either. But I do want you to be happy."

"Me, too," Vera added.

Katherine's heart warmed to hear those closest to her express their fondest wishes for her welfare. "I have discovered that Otis does not hold the key to my happiness."

Father grinned. "I think Christopher is practicing with Katherine more than necessary for a church talent show."

So Father had noticed! Could it be so? "Oh, but it's a complicated number," Katherine explained.

Vera giggled.

"Well, I certainly don't object if he wants to spend a little extra time with you. I've always liked Christopher. I had no idea you weren't interested in Otis. I'm like your mother. I thought the possibility of a courtship was the reason he made the trip up here to start with."

Katherine sighed. "Well, maybe at one time I thought Otis was exciting. And maybe he is. But he just doesn't hold any romantic interest for me. And now that I think about it, I doubt that he ever did."

❧

"Did you enjoy the revival meeting?" Mother asked Otis and Katherine as they talked around the kitchen table after the first meeting.

"Yes. The pastor was wonderful," Otis said.

"But not as wonderful as our pastor," Katherine added.

"I'm glad you didn't make me go," Betsy opined, looking up from her book.

The clock chimed nine times.

"That reminds me," Otis said, "My pocket watch has been running slow. Let me see how it's doing." He reached into his vest pocket. A stricken look crossed his features.

"What's the matter, Otis?" Katherine asked.

He didn't answer right away but patted around his vest pocket. "It's not here."

"What?"

Otis patted more frantically. "My money clip. It's gone!"

"Gone?" Mother asked. "Are you sure you had it?"

"I never leave home without it."

Betsy, Katherine, Otis, and Mother searched the house for the money clip, even eliciting Father's help. The clip was nowhere to be found.

"Someone must have taken it at church," Otis concluded.

"Otis, do you know how ridiculous that sounds? Why would anyone at church take your money clip?" Mother said.

"Why indeed?" Father noted, "Although I'm sure no one at church took it. When did you see it last, Otis?"

"Actually, I didn't have it at church, come to think of it. I slipped my offering in my pants pocket and left my money clip here."

A collective sigh could be heard in the kitchen.

"Let me check my room now." He returned moments later. His face looked pale. "It's not there."

"What do you mean, it's not there?"

"It's not on the table where I left it."

"Then where could it be?"

"I don't have any notion. I must have dropped it somewhere." Katherine could see by Otis's demeanor that he didn't think any of them took it.

"This means you won't be able to leave, right?" Betsy asked, her eyes wide. "Maybe you can stay with us forever?"

"Oh, I think I shall wear out my welcome long before eternity." Otis chuckled. "But I am charmed by your sentiment all the same. Besides, I can always have more money wired."

"Never you mind about that, Otis," Mother said. "You are our guest, and we'll take care of you. One way or another."

"I'm sure we'll resolve this matter soon. Why don't we keep looking? Perhaps I dropped it on the floor."

The family scoured the house to no avail.

"I can't imagine what happened, Otis." Mother said.

"I'm so sorry," Father added.

"No, I beg your pardon for causing you worry," Otis said. "It is far too late now to vex ourselves any longer about it. No doubt the money clip will show itself in the light of day. Maybe in the yard."

"Maybe," Katherine agreed. "I hope so."

❧

The money clip did not show itself in the yard or anywhere else the following day in spite of continued efforts to find it.

"This visit certainly has started to see its share of odd circumstances," Otis noted. "First I find I've been deceived, then my money clip turns up missing. I'm almost afraid to speculate on what might happen next."

"I understand why you're upset, Otis," Katherine told him. "I would be, too, if my money were missing. But there's nothing we can do about it except keep looking and praying."

Otis let out a harrumph. "All the same, I'll send away for funds from home. They should arrive soon."

Despite Otis's grumpy manner, Katherine felt sorry for him. No matter what, he didn't deserve to lose his money. She had an idea what might have happened to it but didn't feel at peace about confronting the person who might have been the perpetrator. That would have to wait until the right time.

The following day, practice for the talent show went well, especially since Otis had decided to grace them with his presence. They ran through their performance several times without any noticeable flaws. For once, Katherine felt as though they might be recognized with a prize at the talent show.

Otis didn't agree. "I noticed we were a little off on the chorus today, and the flaw never was corrected to my satisfaction. I suggest we practice our songs one last time."

Katherine felt too tired, both physically and mentally, to resume playing, but she responded the only gracious way she knew how. "That. . .that seems like a good idea."

Even without Vera present to play along with them, the practice went well.

"I'd say after this session, Otis, you have two excellent chances of winning the competition. You should be proud."

"Hmph. No matter what the outcome, I will share the glory with someone else."

The clacking of heels against hardwood floors greeted them. "Lemonade, anyone?"

Katherine couldn't remember a time when she had been so glad to see her mother. She held a silver tray on which rested drinking glasses and a pitcher of cold beverage.

Mother smiled. "It's such a hot day, I thought you might like some additional refreshment."

Otis took a glass. "Thank you, Mrs. Jones."

Miranda held out her hand to accept a glass. A look of panic crossed her face when she studied her blank wrist. "My bracelet!"

"Bracelet?" Katherine asked.

"It's gone!" Miranda clutched her wrist as if the motion would cause the bracelet to reappear.

Katherine's stomach lurched. She wished there were a doubt as to whether or not Miranda had worn a bracelet, but she knew her friend had indeed included the jewelry in her day's ensemble. She recalled the charms tinkling together when the group met outside before coming into the house to rehearse.

"I can't replace some of the charms I had on that bracelet. I have to find it!" Miranda's voice grew high pitched.

"I'll help you," Otis assured her.

Katherine spotted Betsy playing a game of fetch with Rover. "Have you seen Miranda's bracelet?" she called to her sister.

Betsy watched Rover running with a stick in his mouth, then turned toward Katherine. She shook her head. "No. Why?"

Betsy looked innocent enough, but Katherine approached her while the others searched the house and yard. "It's missing."

"I'm sorry. Do you want me to help you look for it?" Betsy pushed a loose lock of hair off her face and tried to weave it back into her braid.

"You can. Or you can tell me where it is."

Betsy's brown eyes widened. "But I don't know where it is."

"Just like you don't know where Otis's money clip is?"

"Money clip?" She shook her head back and forth rapidly.

"No! I don't! I promise."

Katherine bent down and looked her sister in the eyes. "Betsy, remember the extra money you said you have? Where did it come from?"

She pouted. "I—I saved it up."

"But what about Christmas? I know you don't have a lot of money, and if you keep spending it, even if only two cents at a time, there won't be much left over for gifts."

"Yes, there will. I promise. I'll help you look for the bracelet."

Katherine stopped her. "So you're saying you don't know where the bracelet is?"

"No. I don't."

"Are you sure?"

"Why should I know?"

Katherine didn't know how she could say what she meant. "Well, it's pretty. I know you like it."

"But I wouldn't take it. That's what you're saying, isn't it?"

"No, not really," Katherine protested.

"Yes, you are. I'm not stupid." Hurt filled Betsy's eyes. "I didn't take the bracelet or the money clip. And I never would. I never would take anything that didn't belong to me. I can't believe you would think that!" Tears threatened.

Betsy could be mischievous, but Katherine sensed the child was telling the truth. Betsy had admitted she didn't want Otis to leave, but she didn't fidget or avert her eyes when confronted with the question of the money clip's whereabouts. Nor did she flinch when questioned about Miranda's bracelet. "All right. I believe you. I'm sorry I even asked. You know I love you very much, but even the most wonderful person in the world can be tempted. And you have to understand that we are all concerned. Things are turning up missing around here. Things that shouldn't be. Doesn't it seem strange to you?"

"Yes." Betsy nodded. "But I didn't take anything."

"I know that now. I'm sorry I asked. Can you forgive me?"

Betsy hesitated.

"Pretty please with sugar on top?"

A little smile crossed her lips, and she nodded. "Okay, then."

Katherine hugged her little sister. "So do you have any idea at all what might have happened to Miranda's bracelet?"

"No. I really don't. But I'll help you look."

"It's a deal."

The sisters exchanged an embrace.

They were interrupted when Christopher tapped Katherine on the shoulder. "Hey, aren't you two going to help us look?"

"Of course. Please, Betsy."

Betsy headed in the direction of the driveway.

Obviously picking up on Katherine's tense mood, Christopher asked, "What was that about?"

"I was asking Betsy if she knew anything about the bracelet. I was especially concerned because Otis's money clip went missing the other night."

Christopher's eyes widened. "I wonder how something like that could have happened?"

"I don't know, especially in our own house."

"And you thought Betsy might know something about it?"

"Well, she did want him to stay." She decided not to mention that Betsy wanted their guest to stay forever.

"I don't think Betsy would hide Otis's money clip. And I don't think she's all that interested in Miranda's bracelet."

"Well, she did admire it once, and that made me think of her, but I know now she didn't take either item. Then who did?"

"I don't know. I wish I could solve the mystery." He motioned for her to join him in continuing the search for the bracelet. They both kept their eyes on the ground. "Do you mind if I ask you something?" he inquired a moment later when they were out of earshot of the others.

"No."

"You said Betsy wants Otis to stay. I know he pays attention to her and gives her little gifts, and she's taken to Rover very well. So it's only natural she'd want Otis to stay. But what about you?" His voice softened. "Will you miss Otis when he's gone?"

She didn't answer right away. "Well, I suppose I will. He's a nice enough fellow."

"Oh. But you don't want him to stay on indefinitely?"

"No," she admitted. "Is it that obvious?"

"No, not to anyone but me. You've been nothing but kind to him."

"Well, yes. As I said, I like him well enough, but not as a suitor, if that's what you mean."

"That's what I mean."

Katherine looked up at him and saw a light in his eyes she hadn't seen since Otis's arrival. Could he be feeling the same way about her that she had been feeling about him? It couldn't be possible. Could it?

"Come on," he said, breaking into her thoughts. "Let's see if we can find the lost objects."

eleven

Even after an intense search, they hadn't produced either lost item, but the losses were the last thing on Christopher's mind as he made his way home later.

Katherine is free! Katherine is free!

As he rode home, Christopher whistled, something he hadn't done in a long while. Come to think of it, he hadn't whistled a happy tune since Otis arrived in Maryland.

Christopher had a feeling that Katherine's change of heart had something to do with Miranda. Yes, Otis had been all too forgiving of Miranda and seemingly less tolerant of Katherine's part in the ruse—started by Miranda, no less—than Christopher had thought would be the case once all was revealed. Yet Miranda had flirted her way into Otis's heart, which no doubt explained his response. Christopher had been watching Katherine around Otis since his arrival and noted that she never seemed to warm up to him much. Rover's presence seemed to gain Otis a place in Betsy's heart rather than Katherine's.

Maybe Katherine did love Christopher, after all. Enough not to let another man take away her affections. If only that could be so!

From the looks of things, the way Otis and Miranda stayed near one another during the search, Otis had decided to court Miranda, and she would accept. Christopher wasn't surprised. Miranda and Otis had never missed a chance to converse with one another since they first met.

Christopher harbored no regrets about Otis's visit. Now that Katherine had seen Otis in person and sparks had failed to ignite, she would be more than happy to pursue other interests. His conscience could be clear when he asked Mr. Jones if he would be welcome to court her. He could barely contain himself.

Moments later, after he had put General Lee in his stall for the night, Christopher walked to the house. The tuneless but happy melody still played upon his lips as he bounded up the steps to the verandah.

"Well, I'd say from the sound of that whistlin' of yours that practice went mighty well this afternoon." Grandpa rocked back and forth in his wicker rocking chair, taking advantage of the cool evening air as was his habit.

"Very well. Very well indeed." He decided to share what happened with Grandpa. Stopping in his tracks, he leaned against one of the Greek revival columns. "I do believe Otis and Miranda both have a gleam in their eye for each other. Wouldn't surprise me one little bit to find out they're courting."

"It wouldn't surprise me, either," Grandpa noted.

"You saw the way they act around each other, too?"

The older man resumed rocking. "I think everybody did. Except Otis. Thank the Lord he finally came to his senses. Now you can make your move. Find out what Katherine really thinks of you."

"I will, Grandpa. I will."

Christopher shot through the door and ran up the stairs to the small attic room where he had spent many childhood hours and would remain until his wedding day, when he would take ownership of the parcel of land on the east side of the farm that his father had promised would be his. On that acreage Christopher would build his own little house for his new wife and anticipated family.

He took out the small typewriter and placed it on the well-worn desk from his boyhood, sized for a younger student rather than a man. Placing a piece of paper on the roller, he looked at the blank page.

He typed, "Chapter One."

❧

"That certainly was an uplifting service." Katherine's voice sounded light, as though she had just indulged in a drink of fresh, cool water.

Christopher kept pace beside her as they headed for the buggy. He had been hesitant to ask his father if he could borrow the buggy every night that week. Thankfully, Daddy didn't seem to mind.

"Yes, the sermon was rousing," Christopher agreed. "So rousing I almost forgot the heat."

"On a muggy night like this, I doubt anyone can forget the heat for long." Katherine fanned herself with her Sunday-best fan, a frothy affair with feathers on the handle. She had told him once, some time ago, that the fan had been a gift from a cousin who loved to travel the world. Christopher could see by how Katherine waved it back and forth with such force that she really was trying to cool herself rather than putting on a flirtation for his benefit. "Nor can I forget our troubles," she added. "I wish we could find the money clip and bracelet."

"Me, too. So strange how both disappeared without a trace."

"I don't understand it. But it's a wonder Otis hasn't high-tailed it out of Maryland for good. He must think all of us are liars. First we put on a ruse; then his money clip turns up missing."

"I'm sure he thinks nothing of the sort."

"Still, it's mysterious."

Christopher shrugged. "It's entirely possible that Otis lost his money clip somewhere and Miranda lost her bracelet, too. After all, she's been wearing it for some time, and the latch could have loosened over the course of the afternoon."

"True. But I wish we could find the lost items."

Christopher didn't want to linger on the mystery. Instead, he caught a firefly, making sure not to tighten his palm enough to hurt the bug. Stopping in his stride, he opened his palm and showed his prize to Katherine. The little insect blinked for them once, then twice, before it flew into the darkness.

"You haven't changed a bit." Katherine shook her head as they resumed walking.

"Sure I have. I used to collect them and put them in a jar. With air holes, of course."

"Of course." She giggled.

"Now I just let them go. Isn't that better?"

She laughed. The sound of such joy left Christopher with a warmed heart. How he had missed having Katherine all to himself. Now that Otis had made it a habit to escort Miranda home each night, Christopher felt so light he could have flown to the moon and back, if such a thing had been possible. The fact that Katherine had agreed he could escort her home each evening made his time with her more precious.

With Christopher's assistance, Katherine boarded the buggy. The touch of her warm hand left him with a pleasant tingle. He wished he could prolong the contact, but to try to do so wouldn't be proper. Instead, he made his away around to the other side of the buggy and then leapt onto the seat.

Katherine didn't waste time once the buggy got moving with a jerk and a start. "So, what did you think of the sermon?"

How could he answer? He wanted to hold on to his manly

pride so he didn't admit out loud—even to Katherine—how much the evangelist had touched his soul. Since childhood, he had considered himself a Christian. Yet the minister made him see what Katherine had been telling him all along for so many years. That thankfulness for God's loving care was key to a Christian's joy. He could almost feel his burdens lifted. Suddenly, he knew that everything important in his life would work to God's glory if he surrendered all to Him.

"I found it comforting that he said Jesus will lift my burdens. Just like you said," he conceded.

"Of course it's just like I said." She tilted her chin upward in a self-satisfied manner.

He grinned in amusement, then turned serious. "The pastor has convicted me."

"Really?" Even in the dark, he could see her mouth slacken. "How?"

"You were there years ago when I accepted Christ as my personal savior."

"How well I remember. You're a good man, Christopher Bagley."

A delightful shiver ran up his spine as he sensed the depths of feeling behind her words. "You know, God has been doing all the work in my relationship with Him. He's been listening to my petitions, answering prayer, and walking with me. And I never have hesitated to call on Him in times of trouble."

"Aren't we all quick to call on Him in those times?" Katherine's soft voice sounded tinged with regret.

"I suppose. But He keeps walking with me. Like last night."

"Last night? What happened?"

He hesitated. "I haven't mentioned this to anyone else." He stopped. Would she think him silly?

"You can trust me with any confidence. You know that."

"I think I can." He cleared his throat. "I started on my book. I have almost written the first chapter. Or typed it, rather."

She gasped. "Why, Christopher! That's wonderful! I just knew you'd write that book one day."

"Well, it's hardly written yet." He chuckled.

"I know, but chapter one is a wonderful start! Do tell me what it's about!"

"It's a work of fiction."

"Fiction? I thought you'd write a biography."

"I might. But I want to write a fictional story first. A story of family and what it's like to live here in Maryland."

"Not too exotic," she teased.

"No, but from my heart. And if no one wants to publish it, that's fine. I'll keep it, and my grandchildren can read it one day."

"Grandchildren. The thought seems so far away. But family is something to be thankful for. Maybe you can serve God by focusing at least some of the story on how your characters walk in faith."

He remained pensive for a moment. "Come to think of it, that's a great way to serve Him. Not that I could write a fictional story about the people around here, especially our two families, without mentioning God."

"Amen. He has given us so much."

"That's what the pastor has impressed upon me this week."

"Me, too. I see now that I don't thank Him as often as I should."

"I don't believe it."

"Then I have a proposal for you. Why don't we agree to thank the Lord for three extra things each day? And we'll talk about it every night, being accountable to one another."

He thought for a moment. "That's a wonderful idea. Let's do that."

ﾋ

After bidding Christopher farewell for the evening, Katherine stepped over the threshold and shut the kitchen door behind her.

"Katherine?" Mother called from the sitting room. "Is that you?"

"Yes, ma'am." Katherine ventured in to see her mother. She found her sitting in her rocker. Mother set the book she was reading in her lap and looked up.

"How did the meeting go tonight?" she asked.

Father, sitting in an overstuffed chair beside Mother, looked up from the newspaper crossword puzzle he was in the process of completing. "Was it much like the one last night?"

Katherine nodded. Her parents allowed her to travel to the meeting with Christopher rather than them, a sure sign they didn't mind her spending time with him. "Very much. The pastor was very lively and entertaining."

Father tapped his pencil against the newsprint and looked at Mother. "It sure sounds like he hasn't lost much of his energy or zeal. Maybe we should go."

"Maybe we should. If you don't mind us following you along," Mother teased.

"Mother, how many times do I have to tell you Christopher and I are just friends?"

Katherine's parents exchanged a look. She decided not to ask what they were thinking.

ﾋ

Christopher and Katherine rode in the buggy headed for home after the last night of the revival. Christopher glimpsed at the church one last time as they left the churchyard. The little chapel lacked the stained glass of fine places of worship in the city, but the church held its weight in inspiration. Looking ahead, he watched the sun, only beginning its descent on the horizon, turn the clouds pink, perhaps clothing itself in a soft blanket as it tucked itself in bed for the night. He held back a chuckle. Being around Katherine was causing him to make poetic observations.

He would miss taking Katherine to and from the meetings. On this night, she looked especially pretty, wearing a dress she told him she had sewn just the past week. She had already worn the dress to Monday night's meeting, but he didn't mind seeing it again. None of the women he knew except Miranda could go a whole week without repeating. Besides, mint green went well with Katherine's dark hair.

"A lot of people went up to the altar tonight, didn't they?" Christopher mused.

"Yes. I think this week has been a great success. And we can count it a success, too, since we've been inspired to increase our prayer life. What did you thank God for today?" Katherine asked.

"I thanked Him for the pink blanket He made for the sun."

She peered at the sky. "It is pretty, isn't it?" Then she started. "Why, you didn't thank Him for that today. We're looking at it now."

"I thanked Him just now. Doesn't that count?"

She twisted her lips and cocked her head. "But what about earlier today? What did you thank Him for?"

He didn't hesitate. "You."

"And I thanked Him for you," she admitted. "What else?"

"For enough food to eat and my family."

"Same here."

"We certainly do think alike."

"Yes, but you know, we need to expand. Both of us need to come up with something more original."

"Remember, Solomon said there's nothing new under the sun," Christopher pointed out.

"There's nothing new that God hasn't seen, but we can at least show Him we're thinking beyond the basics. Don't you agree?"

"Yes. I accept your challenge. I'll expand my range of thankfulness tomorrow. And the next day. And the next." A thought occurred to him. "Don't I get any credit for my pink blanket idea just now?"

"Yes, that is pretty original. Especially for a man."

"Hey, what's that supposed to mean? Are you saying men aren't supposed to appreciate a good sunset?"

"No, of course not." She giggled.

Christopher joined her mirth, enjoying their easy rapport.

He brought the team to a stop in front of her house, then after jumping down himself, helped her disembark from the buggy.

Katherine looked at the house and noticed that her parents' bedroom light shone. Otherwise, the house was dark.

"A penny for your thoughts," Christopher prompted.

"Do you think they're worth a penny?" she quipped.

"More than that, I'm sure. So what are you thinking?"

She paused, wondering if she should share. "I'm just speculating on whether Mother will be looking out the window at us shortly."

He chuckled. "No doubt she will be."

"Let her look. There's no place I'd rather be than here with you tonight." She paused.

"I feel exactly the same way."

As he took her in his arms, she became aware of the cinnamon aroma of soap that always hung about him, a pleasant but subtle reminder that he was near. His body near hers felt warm, but despite the heat she didn't mind. As though God read her thoughts, He sent a breeze their way at that moment. The cooling air wafted through her cotton dress.

Christopher grasped her more closely. He gazed into her eyes, and she studied his, lit as they were by the moonlight. He slowly brought his face toward hers. As their lips met, Katherine realized this was a moment she had been waiting for all of her life. She wanted the kiss to last forever.

twelve

The night of the talent competition arrived. Katherine felt as ready to perform as she ever would be. Not that she could concentrate much on the talent show. Her thoughts lingered time and again on Christopher's kiss. Every once in a while, she brought her fingers to her lips, remembering the sweet touch of his lips. She wondered if he thought of the kiss, too.

She hadn't seen Christopher since the night he had kissed her. Her heart pounded with anticipation of seeing him again. She was ready for the show early. Though she tried to appear relaxed, the urge to peer out the window time and again overtook her. Finally, Christopher arrived in his buggy right on time, looking dapper in his dark Sunday suit. She was glad she had decided that night to wear a dress he had said was his favorite—her mint green frock.

Still, for the first time, she felt awkward in his presence. "Are you ready for the show?" Her question sounded weak to her ears, as though she were trying to make conversation where there was none.

"Yes." His terse response wasn't characteristic of him, either.

Christopher must have thought the kiss was a mistake. Or is he just feeling awkward? We have been friends for so long. Will romance be easy for us?

As Christopher helped her onto the buggy, Katherine noticed once more how manly his strong hand, roughened from farm work, felt on hers. She wanted him to linger in the touch, but as soon as she was seated, he hastened to take his place beside her. His posture looked stiff rather than shouting the easygoing confidence to which she had become accustomed from him. "I promised Vera I'd take her as well. So we'll be going by her house next."

Katherine nodded. Maybe the fact that they planned to pick up Vera on the way would help. Her company would surely ease the awkwardness.

She eyed a boy riding up the driveway on a horse that was black as midnight. "Look! It's a stable hand from the Sharpe farm."

Christopher brought the buggy to a halt. "He seems to be in a hurry."

"Is everything alright?" Katherine asked the stable hand as soon as he drew within earshot.

"I think so. I have a message for you, Miss Jones." He handed her a missive written on Vera's ivory-colored stationery.

Nervous, Katherine opened the letter and read aloud:

My dearest Katherine,
*   Forgive me, but Alice's time to deliver her baby has come, and I must tend to her. I am so sorry I cannot play the harp with you at the show tonight. I have summoned the midwife, but I don't expect the baby to arrive before morning. I will send news of the baby's birth. Please put on your performance without me. I know you are sure to do me proud!*

*   With love from your faithful friend,*
*   Vera*

"Oh Christopher, I don't think we'll win without her."

"We're not there to win. We're there to be a part of the evening," Christopher reminded Katherine.

"Yes, I suppose you're right." She grimaced and folded the missive.

At that moment, Mother and Father hurried out of the house.

"What is it, Katherine?" Mother wanted to know. "Is everything alright?"

"I hope so. Alice's baby is coming. The midwife should be there by now." A worried tone entered her voice. "I didn't think she was due to deliver for another two weeks."

"Give or take two weeks is perfectly fine," Mother assured her. "Predicting such things as the birth of a baby isn't an exact science, you know. The details of life are best left to God."

"Yes, I have learned that more than ever recently," Katherine noted. "But I do wish the baby had waited a little longer. Just a few hours. Vera's harp added so much to our song."

"I doubt the baby knows anything about your harp music," Father teased.

"True." Katherine smiled.

"Will you still perform in the show?" Mother asked.

"Yes. We'll give it out best try," Christopher answered.

Katherine knew what she needed to do. "Father, will you lead us in prayer for Alice's baby?"

"I thought you'd never ask." He prayed for Alice's health, the baby's safe arrival and future, and for Alice and Elmer as they would become new parents on that night.

A cloak of silence embraced them as they contemplated Father's prayer.

Mother broke the silence. "If the two of you are planning to be on time for the show, you'll need to get going!"

"So we shall." Christopher smiled and tipped his hat in the direction of Katherine's mother.

"We'll see you there," Father said.

"And we'll be rooting for you," Mother added.

"Thanks!" Katherine waved at her parents as the buggy left the yard.

The horses trotted well and swiftly. Once they arrived at church, Christopher unharnessed his horses and took a moment to feed the faithful beasts a sugar cube apiece. He patted General Lee on the nose. "There's more of this where that came from, fella."

The steed whinnied.

Katherine turned and saw Mrs. Watkins standing near the entrance to the sanctuary. She motioned for them to come closer, using quick little movements that bespoke urgency. "She seems like she wants to see us in a hurry. Let's go."

When they met Mrs. Watkins, they could see the expression she wore wasn't happy.

Christopher tipped his hat at the older woman. "Good evening, Mrs. Watkins."

After they finished exchanging greetings, Katherine couldn't stand the suspense. "If I may mention it, you look a bit upset, Mrs. Watkins. Is everything alright?" A terrible thought occurred to her. "You. . .you didn't hear that anything untoward has happened to Alice, did you?"

Mrs. Watkins's eyes widened behind her spectacles. "Alice? Alice Sharpe?"

"Yes, ma'am."

"Oh, no. Why?"

"She's delivering her baby tonight," Katherine informed her.

Mrs. Watkins gasped. "Already? I just can't believe how time flies."

"Yes, ma'am. Vera sent us a message. She'll be with Alice and won't be performing with us." Katherine sent Mrs. Watkins a pleading look. "I hope we can still be in the show."

"Oh, certainly. Certainly." Mrs. Watkins nodded. "That shouldn't present a problem. Although Vera is so sweet and talented. I'm sorry she'll be missing out on this opportunity to perform for us."

"Me, too."

"What I have to tell you does concern the show, however," Mrs. Watkins said. "The chairman looked over the finalized roster of performers and decided at the last minute to make a change in the rules. That change affects you."

Katherine held her breath, even though she wasn't surprised by the chairman's actions. Mr. Perkins was a known grump, and he seemed to take pleasure in creating the greatest amount of uproar over the smallest details.

"When he looked over the roster, Mr. Perkins noted that Otis was participating in two acts. Were you aware of that?"

Both nodded. "We were told that would be fine," Christopher elaborated.

"It would have been, had I been in charge. But I'm afraid Mr. Perkins sees things differently. When he noticed that Otis was participating in two acts, he ruled that in fairness to the rest of the competition, Otis could only perform once."

"Does Otis know this?" Katherine asked.

"Yes, and that's where you come in. I asked him what we should do, and he has chosen not to accompany you but Miss Miranda Henderson."

"Oh," was all Katherine could manage to say.

"I'm so sorry," Mrs. Watkins said. "I wish there was something I could do, but I'm afraid my hands are tied."

"That's fine, Mrs. Watkins," Katherine assured her. "We're glad you told us as soon as you could."

She smiled, and her posture softened with obvious relief. "Thank you for being so cooperative. Of course, I would expect as much from two of my best Sunday school students."

"Yes, ma'am," Christopher and Katherine responded in unison.

"Well, I must be moving along. Lots to do, you know." She scurried into the social hall.

Left with Christopher, Katherine noticed that although he hadn't said much to Mrs. Watkins, he wore a dark expression.

He shook his head. "If that doesn't beat everything I've ever seen. Leaving us stranded like that."

She searched for consolation. "Otis can't be blamed for his decision."

Christopher crossed his arms. "Is that so?"

"Not entirely. I concede that perhaps he can be faulted for choosing to perform with Miranda instead of us. After all, he had made a pledge that he would play the piano with our act." She hurried to add, "But he apparently also made a promise to Miranda. And he was put in an untenable position at the last minute. What could he really do? After all, you and I are performing together, whereas without him, Miranda would be all alone. And he had no way of knowing that Alice's baby would come tonight so Vera wouldn't be performing with us."

"True. But I still say he's a snake."

Katherine laughed. The sound of her mirth brought a sideways grin to Christopher's face.

"I can see it's just you and me, then."

Why did that sound so good? "Yes," Katherine said. "It's just you and me."

"And together, we'll do just fine."

"Yes. Together, we'll do just fine."

"Are we changing our act so that you're now a parrot?" Christopher teased.

Katherine caught on without hesitation. "Are we changing our act so you're now a parrot?" She mimicked a squawk. "Polly want a cracker!" She let out two sharp whistles.

Christopher laughed. "That's pretty good. Maybe we should change our act after all."

"Unh-uh. I think you should sing instead. I just hope my solo accompaniment can do you justice."

"Sure it will."

"Just in case, let's sneak into the Harvesters classroom and do a quick run-through on the piano. Shall we?"

"We shall."

After going through the song twice, Katherine was pleased. "Well! That doesn't sound quite as horrid with my playing alone as I anticipated.

Christopher chuckled. "You always could cheer me up."

She giggled.

"Now let's go in there and knock 'em dead."

"Christopher! I'm not sure that's what we should really say about a church performance," she teased.

"At least we'll all be headed to a good place," he countered.

She shook her head and sent him a lopsided grin. "You're incorrigible."

"From you, I'll take that as a compliment."

"That you may."

Their mood lightened, Katherine and Christopher were prepared to enjoy the talent show. They sat in the audience near the front along with the other participants. Betsy sat beside them. She twiddled her thumbs and rocked back and forth, a sure sign she was nervous.

Katherine looked for Miranda and Otis but saw neither of them. She decided to concentrate on the notes she would need to play so their act could be a success.

Soon the strong scent of lily of the valley drifted Katherine's way from behind, a scent that always hung about Miranda. Katherine felt a tap on her shoulder. She turned to see Miranda.

Miranda tightened her lips, and a light of regret emitted from her eyes. "Did Mrs. Watkins see you?"

Katherine nodded.

Miranda sighed. "I'm sorry about your act. Otis didn't want to let you down, but he didn't feel he had any other choice."

To confirm Miranda's proclamation, Katherine caught a glimpse of Otis. Indeed, he looked sheepish and sent her an apologetic shrug. Remembering what she had told Christopher as well as her resolve to act with kindness toward Otis, Katherine made sure no disappointment displayed itself on her features.

"Will you still be performing?" Miranda's concern seemed genuine.

Katherine nodded. "Don't worry. Christopher and I can make do, but without Otis, you would have been much worse off than we would, with no accompaniment at all."

Miranda's body relaxed with obvious relief. "And besides, you have Vera. Where is she, anyway?"

"Uh, we don't have Vera. She's with Alice. The baby is coming soon. Sometime tonight."

Miranda gasped but followed with an enthusiastic, "Oh, how exciting!" before Mrs. Watkins shushed the audience.

Katherine turned toward the stage and watched the performances. She wasn't disappointed. All of the acts were entertaining, and many were executed with professional competence.

As the show progressed, Katherine speculated silently on which act might win the blue ribbon and, as an added incentive, a certificate for two free dinners at the Hagerstown Inn. Katherine thought surely four-year-old Mary Lou, with her moppish dash of blond ringlets, was a shoo-in with her ballet performance. But after seeing Jim Bob's unicycle and juggling act, she decided maybe Mary Lou would have to be content with the red ribbon and bag of penny candy. Surely a little girl would prefer a sack of sweets to a meatloaf dinner, anyway. Then again, who could ignore the outrageously funny skit that several of the high schoolers presented? She was only glad she could sit on the sidelines and not be called upon to judge.

Next followed Betsy and her tap dance. Katherine whispered encouraging words to her before she took her turn. Christopher winked, and she giggled in return.

Dressed in light blue with a large matching bow, her dark hair fashioned in sausage curls, she rivaled Mary Lou in attractiveness. Even better, she performed a flawless rendition of her tap dance, hitting each note just right. Mother was in fine form with her accompaniment as well. After the song, Betsy curtsied prettily, curls falling back into perfect place. Her smile made her look like a seasoned performer. Katherine couldn't remember a time she had been prouder of her little sister. The audience clapped and whistled.

Later, Miranda sang her aria without missing a note. Otis delivered a performance on the piano that expressed the emotion of the music in a flawless fashion. The conclusion of their number was greeted by applause so great that Katherine thought the building might burst.

She felt nervous now that their turn was nigh, but Katherine knew that singing to God's glory took first place. The money raised from the sales of tickets was to be donated to a nearby orphanage in the name of the church and of Jesus Christ. How much more glory and honor could there be?

Mr. Perkins rose from his seat and took center stage, as he

did between each act. He clapped along with the audience until their applause ceased. Mr. Perkins then launched into his introduction. "And now, ladies and gentlemen, we come to our last act for this evening. Miss Katherine Jones and Mr. Christopher Bagley will be performing a medley of song for our entertainment and enjoyment. Please give them a warm welcome!" He clapped, and the audience followed suit.

Katherine felt self-conscious as she took to the stage. She almost wished she hadn't worn her conspicuous mint green dress. She glanced at Christopher, who stood straight, gazing upon the audience as though they were in for a great treat.

She suppressed a smile. Christopher really was a performer!

She scooted onto the piano bench and unfolded her sheet of music.

"Good evening, ladies and gentlemen," Christopher said. "Tonight it is my distinct pleasure to perform a popular melody known as 'The Blue and the Gray' or 'A Mother's Gift to Her Country' written by Paul Dresser."

Christopher nodded to let Katherine know he was ready to begin singing. She played a brief introduction. He sang in a perfect baritone, hitting every note with precision:

> "A mother's gift
> To her country's cause
> Is a story yet untold.
> She had three sons,
> Three only sons,
> Each worth his weight in gold.
> She gave them up
> For the sake of war,
> While her heart was filled with pain.
> As each went away,

She was heard to say,
He will never return again.

"One lies down near Appomattox,
Many miles away.
Another sleeps at Chickamauga
And they both wore suits of gray.
'Mid the strains of 'Down to Dixie'
The third was laid away
In a trench at Santiago.
The Blue and the Gray.

"She's alone tonight,
While the stars shine bright,
With a heart full of despair.
On the last great day
I can hear her say,
My three boys will be there.
Perhaps they'll wait
At the heav'nly gates,
On guard beside their guns.
Then the mother true,
To the gray and blue,
May enter with her sons."

Katherine could hear a few sobs and sniffles from the audience as she played, but she dared not look up lest she miss a note. Moments later as she took her bow, Katherine couldn't see a woman in the house who could boast a dry eye. Mrs. Watkins shook with sobs. Mr. Boyd blew his nose with a hearty snort into a red bandana. Katherine wasn't surprised. The citizens of the region had been greatly impacted by the War Between the

States and the recent conflict in Cuba.

Christopher sent Katherine a slight nod, prompting her to play the first chords of "Dixie." Without a moment's hesitation, the crowd stood in respect to the anthem of the Confederacy. By the time he had completed the last chorus, all the men seemed to be holding back tears. Everyone seemed to remember the losses, the bravery, the horrible realities of war. Hitting the last note, Katherine knew that no matter what the outcome, they could not have performed better that evening.

But victory didn't matter. Her reward was Christopher's smile. He motioned for her to join him by his side. Katherine curtsied; then he took a bow. Applause resounded in wave after wave. Katherine eyed the judges conferring. As she and Christopher returned to their seats, she knew the decision would soon be announced.

As the judges continued in their deliberations, each person who participated in the show was invited by Mrs. Watkins and Mr. Perkins to go back up front and take bows to fresh rounds of recognition for their hard work and valiant efforts.

Katherine eyed her parents sitting near the back, dressed in their Sunday best. They sat near Mr. and Mrs. Bagley, dressed in their Sunday finery as well. All four parents clapped as though they'd seen a professional production in New York instead of their own children performing in the little church they'd visited weekly their whole lives. Then again, maybe pride in their own children and the fact that Christopher and Katherine had performed well before people who cared about them all was the reason for the older people's enthusiasm. Certainly Christopher and Katherine's act was more meaningful to their parents than any big production staged by strangers would have been.

Katherine eyed Christopher's grandfather sitting as far up

front as he could, right behind the performers. He looked younger than his years in his Sunday suit, and he wore a yellow rose in his buttonhole. No doubt he had plucked the special bloom himself from Mrs. Bagley's flower garden. She let out a giggle as the elderly gentleman, a veteran of the War Between the States, filled the room with the noise of a shrill and approving whistle.

Mr. Perkins nodded for all to return to their seats and then took the white envelope from the nearest judge. With an exaggerated gesture, he polished the lenses of his reading spectacles. The audience watched as though the action were the most fascinating thing one could ever witness. After he positioned his glasses in their proper position on his thin nose, he extracted a silver letter opener from his vest pocket. He sliced open the missive with a careful gesture. Clearly relishing his role as announcer, he placed the opener back in his pocket and with a flourish extracted a piece of white paper from the envelope. When Mr. Perkins looked over the results, Katherine thought he might make the announcement then. She held her breath.

Instead, he folded the paper, held it in his hand, and spoke to the audience. "I am happy to announce that there are no ties for any of the positions. The judges have reached decisive verdicts on all counts." He grinned at the judges, and they nodded. "First of all, let me say that everyone here tonight is a winner. I think we as their audience have demonstrated our appreciation and sentiments by our vigorous applause."

"Hear, hear!" a man shouted, amid a chorus of new praise.

Mr. Perkins nodded as a signal for the audience to quiet themselves. "Now to announce the winner of our honorable-mention ribbon."

Whispers of speculation could be heard rippling across the audience.

He paused and then looked over the performers sitting in the front part of the audience. "Honorable mention goes to Miss Betsy Jones for her marvelous dance!"

The audience clapped in approval. Betsy pouted with disappointment at coming in so far from first place but saw Mother's chastening look and quickly formed her lips into a winning smile. She took her ribbon with a curtsy and returned to her seat.

"Very fine. Very fine." He cleared his throat. "And moving right along now, our fourth-place winner is—Mr. Jim Bob Boyd and his amazing unicycle!"

Jim Bob sauntered up to accept the ribbon. The semi-frown he wore demonstrated his lack of enthusiasm for his prize. Nevertheless, he nodded toward the audience and mumbled thanks to them and to the judges before he returned to his seat.

"Thank you, Jim Bob, for a fine performance." Mr. Perkins cleared his throat. "And now for our third-place winner. The yellow ribbon is awarded to a vocal performance."

Katherine took in a breath and prepared to go up to the stage to accept the ribbon. With such fierce competition, she and Christopher were lucky to be recognized with a ribbon at all. And a yellow ribbon would look nice in her room, reminding her of a successful evening.

She sent Christopher a little smile, which he returned. He shifted in his seat. Surely he had come to the same conclusion as she and was preparing to accept his ribbon.

"And the yellow ribbon is awarded to—Miss Miranda Henderson for her rendition of 'Havanaise' from the first act of the opera Carmen!"

It took Katherine a moment to recover from the surprise announcement. She settled back in her seat and clapped, stunned. She watched Otis and Miranda rise and stride toward

Mr. Perkins to accept the ribbon.

After they arrived upon the stage, Mr. Perkins presented the prize to Miranda as Otis remained positioned beside, yet still slightly behind, her. Composed as always, Miranda curved her mouth into a pleasing expression that would have led the casual observer to believe she had been awarded the first-place trophy and ribbon. Though pleasant, Otis's grin looked tighter and more constrained than Miranda's. Katherine knew him well enough to realize he was doing his best to conceal disappointment.

Both Miranda and Otis emitted a hearty round of thanks to the audience and to the judges before taking their seats. Katherine had a chance to whisper congratulations to the couple before Mr. Perkins resumed making the announcements.

Katherine relaxed. Since Miranda and Otis placed so low, there was no chance she and Christopher would be recognized. She could enjoy vicarious victory for a friend instead. The pressure was off.

"We're getting closer and closer to announcing the evening's winner, folks!" Mr. Perkins teased.

Katherine refrained from shaking her head. Any other day of the week, Mr. Perkins seemed to revel in his reputation as a grouch. Tonight, he clearly enjoyed playing the part of the jolly announcer. "I must say, I am in wholehearted agreement with this next decision. Our next winner deserves the bag of penny candy from Dooley's Dry Goods Store and her big red ribbon."

Speculative whispers filled the room.

Mr. Perkins continued. "Who can forget such a sweet rendition of the art of ballet? May I see little Miss Mary Lou Evans?"

Mary Lou giggled and bounded up to the stage. Mr. Perkins held out both the red ribbon and the sack of candy to the little girl. She ignored the ribbon and grabbed the candy.

Amid chuckles and "Ahs" from the audience, she pulled on the string, trying to open the bag. Her mother rushed up to retrieve the little girl, the candy, and the ribbon. Mrs. Evans smiled and instructed Mary Lou to thank everyone, which she did in prompt obedience. The pair exited the stage amid laughter and new applause.

"She certainly deserves that big bag of candy, doesn't she, folks?" Mr. Perkins prodded.

More chuckles and applause ensued.

Mr. Perkins gazed over the audience and sent them his broadest smile. "And now for the big moment, folks. The award of the blue ribbon and this lovely engraved trophy." He studied the engraving on the silver loving cup and read, "In Recognition for the Finest Performance of 1901, Blessed Assurance Church Talent Show, Organized by the Ladies Missionary Society in Support of the Kent County Alms House, First Prize for a Talent Performance."

The audience applauded.

"This seems like a fine moment to thank the Ladies' Missionary Society for staging an evening of superb entertainment for us all. Ladies, will you please stand?"

Mrs. Watkins and the rest of her contingent stood and accepted their accolades.

After the clapping died down, Mr. Perkins looked inside the cup. "And not only will the first place winners have this lovely cup to keep forever, but in appreciation for the efforts of the grand-prize winners, the Hagerstown Inn has included a voucher for two fine dinners!"

He paused, and on cue, everyone applauded.

"Now, is everyone ready to hear who will be our grand-prize winners for this evening?"

Shouts of yes filled the room.

"Then don't let me keep you waiting any longer." He took in a breath. "I am pleased to say that this fine prize goes to Mr. Christopher Bagley for his fine performance of 'The Blue and the Gray' and 'Dixie'!"

As even more applause thundered, Katherine gasped. She knew Christopher had outdone himself, and she hadn't made any mistakes in her accompaniment. Yet she had no idea he would walk away with the prize.

"Now that we have those dinner vouchers, we have an excuse for a night out." Christopher winked.

Katherine moved aside so he could receive his award, but he took her hand, insisting that she receive the award along with him.

After they took to the stage and bowed before the audience, Katherine noted that even Otis and Miranda appeared to be pleased with the outcome of the contest. When Mary Lou waved to them, a red, sugarcoated gumdrop was pinched between her forefinger and thumb.

thirteen

The night air felt refreshing against Katherine's face as she and Christopher made their way to the buggy after the show. Stars winked at them from a cloudless sky.

"Were you surprised we won?" she ventured as the buggy pulled out of the church lot.

"A little. I didn't think I was the best singer there tonight."

"I thought you were. If anything, my poor accompaniment dragged you down."

"Now I know you're fishing for compliments since everyone around thinks you're marvelous at the piano."

She giggled. "Okay, maybe I wouldn't mind the occasional compliment. Is that so bad?"

"I suppose not." His sigh was one of contentment. "This night can't get much better."

"Yes, this time has certainly been one filled to the brim with excitement. Probably more excitement than I've seen in my lifetime."

"Maybe things will slow down and get back to normal soon."

"I hope so. I think." Katherine grinned.

They approached the turnoff to the Sharpes' farm. "Do you think we should stop by and see how Alice is doing?"

Katherine hesitated. "I doubt the baby has had time to arrive yet." She looked longingly at the house.

"Come on, Sadie. Giddup, General Lee," Christopher clicked his tongue and pulled the reins to instruct the horses to turn left.

"I can't believe you're doing this."

"I know you can't stand the suspense. Besides, if the baby hasn't been born yet, we'll just go on home," he said. "Alice won't know we've been by, but I'm sure Vera will be glad we stopped in to check on the family."

"I'm sure Elmer is nervous, too," Katherine observed. "After tonight, he'll be a father."

Moments later they pulled in front of the house. Katherine jumped off the buggy, holding the loving cup all the while.

A ragged-looking Vera answered their knock on the back door.

"Uh, oh. It looks like you're still in the middle of everything," Katherine observed. "I guess we shouldn't have stopped by this late. Tell Alice I'm sorry we disturbed all of you."

Vera waved them into the kitchen, shaking her head. "You're not bothering us. The baby arrived just minutes ago." She kept her voice low.

"That's wonderful!" Katherine gasped. "Tell us! Is it a boy or girl?"

"It's a boy." Vera beamed. "They named him Paul Victor."

"Small victory?" Christopher asked only half jokingly.

Katherine thought for a moment. "That's right. *Small* is the meaning of the apostle's name."

"I hadn't thought of that, and I'm not sure Alice did, either." Vera's facial expression looked thoughtful.

"I'm sure throughout his life he'll enjoy triumphs both large and small," Christopher remarked.

"Aw, what a sweet thought." Katherine smiled.

"I think I'll share that with Alice," Vera said. "Once she wakes up, that is."

"Speaking of sleep, we'd better let the proud new aunt get some shut-eye." Katherine tugged on Christopher's sleeve. "Let's go."

"You'll do no such thing!" Vera stopped them with her voice.

"Huh?" Christopher asked.

"Not without telling me about that trophy."

"Oh. This." Katherine had been so involved with the conversation that she had forgotten she was holding a rather cumbersome prize.

"You won, I see." Vera beamed.

Katherine nodded.

"You don't seem too happy."

"Oh, we are," Katherine assured her. "You know something? Winning a prize seemed so monumental only moments ago, but in light of a new birth, a talent show seems inconsequential."

"Inconsequential or not, I am so sorry I left you out in the cold at the last minute," Vera apologized. "But obviously, you didn't need me."

"Yes, we did need you. But we both realize your absence couldn't be helped," Christopher said.

"That's right. We both wish you could have been there. You worked just as hard as the rest of us."

"So tell me all the details." Vera became breathless with anticipation.

"First of all, Mrs. Watkins greeted us at the door with a terrible surprise," Katherine explained.

"Oh?"

"Otis was snatched out from under us."

"Well, not exactly snatched." Christopher told Vera the story.

"I can't say that I blame Otis," Katherine admitted. "Miranda would have been all alone without him."

"True," Vera said. "Oh, I feel so terrible. Even worse now."

"Silly goose! Would you have me blame little Paul for putting us through so much trouble?" Katherine joked.

"So tell me who else won."

Katherine decided to have a little fun by dragging out the anticipation. "Betsy won honorable mention."

"Good for her!"

"She was a little disappointed, I have to admit."

"There's always next year," Vera said.

"That's what I told her," Christopher said.

"Jim Bob took fourth with his unicycle and juggling act."

"Mm-hm."

"Miranda and Otis took third."

Vera's eyes widened. "She just took third place? I can't believe it! What happened? Did Otis flub on the piano?"

"No, we can't lay the blame at Otis's feet—or should I say, hands," Christopher quipped.

Katherine chuckled. "I admit, I was shocked. Her voice is so beautiful, and I've never heard an opera number that she couldn't execute with great success."

"I concur," said Vera. "So who took second?"

Christopher answered. "Mary Lou. She danced a ballet piece."

"Aw, I'll bet that was the sweetest sight!"

Katherine nodded. "And you know who took first prize!"

Vera clapped as though she had just heard the news for the first time.

Christopher finally intervened, speaking in a hushed tone. "Ladies! Do you want to wake the baby?"

Vera looked embarrassed, and Katherine stopped in midbob. "Sorry."

"It's hard to believe we do finally have a baby to consider after all these months of waiting." Vera held her voice to a loud whisper. "I'm so happy for you. See, you didn't need me after all."

"I missed you, though." Katherine waited for Christopher to concur. When he didn't take the hint, she poked him in the ribs as inconspicuously as possible.

"Oh, yes. I missed you, too."

"It's a sin to tell a fib," Vera reminded him, although she sent him a half grin. "You two make a great team. Why can't you see that? Do I have to be the one to tell you?"

"You don't have to be the one to tell us," Christopher responded, "but I don't mind hearing it." He looked into Katherine's eyes.

"All right, you two lovebirds. Time to be on your way. Some of us have real responsibilities." With a waving motion of both hands, Vera shooed them toward the door.

Katherine covered her face and pretended to be fearful of Vera's mock ire. Yet she couldn't resist one keen observation as she exited over the threshold. "One day it will be your turn, Vera."

The blond shrugged. "I'm in no hurry. All in the Lord's good time." Sending the couple a smile, Vera shut the door behind them, but Katherine glanced back in time to catch a wistful look on her friend's face.

Katherine turned to Christopher. "You know, I do hope she finds someone soon. She deserves someone of her own."

"She's helping with little Paul. That should be enough to keep her hands full. And her sister's bound to appreciate what she's doing."

"Of course Vera's appreciated. But I'd like to see her have her own family. She'd be a great mother. If only some man could see it."

"Women! You and your matchmaking!" Christopher looked to the sky and back, shaking his head. "No bachelor is safe around any of you."

"And that's the way it's supposed to be." With her hand in Christopher's, Katherine leapt to her seat.

They passed two neighboring farms, the silence interrupted only by jangling harness and plodding hoofs. They soon arrived at the Joneses' farm. Katherine enjoyed being by Christopher's side to the extent that she was sorry to arrive home.

"Oh, I meant to ask but forgot in all the excitement," Christopher said. "Did you find the missing money clip? Or the bracelet?"

"No, and even worse, I'm missing an earring as well. I could have sworn I left the pair on my dressing table, but I can only find one now."

"That's too bad."

"Yes, and it was my favorite, too. I just can't imagine why someone would take all those trinkets. We've never had this problem before."

"Maybe Otis pretended his money clip was missing so no one would suspect him when he took Miranda's charm bracelet. As a memento of her, of sorts."

Katherine knew Christopher didn't mean what he said. "If Miranda were a real schemer, she might have taken Otis's money clip and then pretended her bracelet was missing. But of course, she would never do such a thing." Katherine sighed. "Neither Miranda or Otis is the culprit, I'm sure. We're grasping at straws."

"Too bad Sherlock Holmes isn't around to help us out."

"I'm sure he could unravel the mystery. But more likely, it's no mystery at all. Just carelessness on Otis's part to make him misplace his money clip. And perhaps a loose clasp on Miranda's bracelet. My earring could have fallen off because of a faulty clip. Who would need only one earring?"

"True."

"It's coincidence. That's all." She thought for a moment. "I've already confronted Betsy, and she told me she didn't take anything. I apologized for thinking it was her."

"So you believe her." Christopher's tone showed he saw no reason not to believe Betsy.

"Yes. But the other day she had extra money, and I never got a satisfactory answer as to how. And she has always admired Miranda's bracelet. Asked about a certain charm, even."

Both of them sat in uncomfortable silence until they arrived at the Joneses' farm. Still, Katherine didn't want the evening to end. She noticed the light was on, an indication that her parents had arrived home first.

After Christopher walked her to the front door, she thought of a stalling tactic, a way to keep him near her a few more moments. "Mother made apple pie today. Would you care to join me for a slice?"

"I reckon I would. I seldom get to eat dessert at my house. You know, apple pie—or any pie, for that matter—doesn't last long with Grandpa around."

"Better get some of that dessert while you can then." She winked.

Just then the front door opened and out bounded Rover. The dog nearly knocked them both down.

"Now scoot, Rover!" Father called after the dog. "No more getting in the house!"

"Aww, poor dog!" Katherine sympathized.

"Poor dog, nothing. He knows better." Father pointed out.

Katherine watched the dog exit to the side yard.

"Come on in, kids," Father offered, holding open the door. He glanced at the loving cup Katherine held and let out a low whistle. "I have to say, that's something!"

"Yes, I wanted you and Mother to see it up close, but I'm going to let Christopher keep it. After all, he's the one who charmed the audience with his singing."

"I think you should keep it, Katherine." Christopher offered.

"I'll hear nothing of the sort."

Christopher grinned. "Oh, all right." He glimpsed at the side yard. "Uh, if you'll excuse me, sir, I want to see something."

"Of course."

Katherine watched as Christopher kept his eyes on the dog. "What's wrong?"

"I'm not sure, but I think I saw something in Rover's mouth. Let's follow him and see what he does." Christopher didn't wait for her to respond but hurried after the collie.

"What do you think is the matter?" Father asked.

She handed him the loving cup. "I don't know, but I'm going to find out." Katherine followed Christopher.

An instant later, both of them watched as the dog dug a hole and dropped a shiny object into it. He was just about to cover it up when Christopher shooed him aside. He bent over and took out a shiny silver spoon. He held it up for Katherine to see. "Well, look at that."

"Mother won't be happy to see her good spoon out here in the dirt."

"A little soap and water will take care of that. But more important, see those little mounds of fresh dirt?" He motioned to several areas. "It looks like Rover's been busy. I have a feeling I know what's in most of those holes."

Katherine suddenly had a feeling, too.

"Would you bring me a lantern and your mother's gardening shovel?"

"Of course!" Katherine hurried to the shed and retrieved both objects.

Christopher was petting and consoling the dog upon her return. She handed him the tool and lit the lantern. Feeling sorry for the animal, she petted him as Christopher dug. Rover barked in protest at having his treasures disturbed, but as Katherine smoothed his fur and spoke to him in sympathetic tones, he calmed himself.

As Christopher plowed into the dirt, he found several shiny objects. Otis's money clip, with the money still attached, Miranda's bracelet, and Katherine's earring were among them. The items bore bits of dirt as testimony to their adventure but otherwise were in pristine condition.

"What a relief!" Katherine placed her hand to her chest. "But that still doesn't explain Miranda's bracelet. She never took it off while she was in the house."

"Let me see something." Christopher tried the clasp. As soon as he shut it, the clutch fell open once more. "See? It's just as I suspected. The clasp was weak. Miranda must have lost it."

"And Rover found it."

"Maybe she'll thank him."

Just then Otis arrived from escorting Miranda home. Katherine and Christopher called out to him.

"Look. We found your money clip." Katherine held up the prize.

"Marvelous!" Otis's grin nearly reached the sides of his face. "And Miranda's bracelet?"

Katherine held up the sparkling bangle. "Right here. And my earring, too."

"So we finally know why the dog was so eager to get in the house," Otis observed. "He wanted to get his clutches on anything shiny."

"Apparently so," Katherine agreed. "Now we'll have to be

serious about keeping him outside or at least well supervised at all times if he does happen to venture indoors."

"I'm sorry my gift has caused so much disturbance," Otis said.

"Don't be sorry. I love Rover, and so does Betsy." Katherine sighed. "Betsy. I asked her if she took the money clip. I feel so terrible about that now."

"Betsy?" Otis asked. "What made you think of her?"

"Well, she had extra money for no reason, and she always liked Miranda's bracelet."

"Extra money? Oh." Otis looked down at the ground and back.

"Why, yes." Katherine grew suspicious. "You wouldn't know anything about that, would you?"

Otis's mouth formed a regretful line and he winced. "I'm afraid I do."

fourteen

Katherine looked at Otis in surprise and noticed that Christopher wore a similar look of disbelief. How could Otis know anything about Betsy and her extra money? Surely he had given her gifts from time to time but always in front of the adults. Besides, he had advised her to save her pennies each time. So what could he mean?

Christopher was quick to take up the line of questioning. "So you were giving her money. Why?"

"She was doing me a favor."

"A favor?"

"She was, uh, delivering letters to Miranda for me. I paid her a nickel for each letter she delivered."

"Oh!" Katherine blurted.

Otis took Katherine's hands in his. "I'm so sorry, Katherine. I must admit I had thoughts first along that we might court. But then I met Miranda, and I felt an inexplicable connection to her. Like we are kindred spirits. Not that I don't think you are a fine woman. You are. Any man would be happy to have you as a wife."

"Any man but you," Katherine teased and then turned serious just as quickly. "I know, Otis. You have no need to apologize to me. I have enjoyed our correspondence, and I will always be glad you and I are acquaintances. But like you, I feel no longing beyond that."

"Thank you. I hope you are not upset with me for partaking of your family's kind hospitality all this time."

"Of course not. You have been a blessing. And I think it was God's plan for you to find Miranda. I've never seen her happier."

Otis beamed.

Father approached the group. "What's going on out here?"

Christopher showed him the holes the dog had dug.

"Rover was our thief," Katherine said. "He's the one who took the money clip, the bracelet, and my earring."

"He had just taken off with this spoon, but we caught him red-pawed," Christopher added.

The group chuckled.

Father whistled. "I was so eager to get him out of the house, I didn't even see the spoon. Well, I'd say this calls for a celebration. In the form of delicious apple pie."

"I'll say," Christopher agreed. "Just let me get these holes filled back in, and I'll be right there."

"I'll stay here and hold the lantern," Katherine offered.

Father agreed, and he and Otis went back into the house.

A few moments later, Katherine and Christopher went back into the house, where the promised pie awaited them.

"I understand you found all our treasures," Mother noted.

"Yes. We've got to keep the dog out of the house." Katherine chuckled. She remembered that she wanted to apologize to her sister. "Where's Betsy?"

"She's gone to bed. It's been a big night."

"Do you think she's asleep yet?"

"I doubt it. Why?"

"I just want to go up and speak to her a minute." Katherine excused herself and made her way to Betsy's room. She had shut off her bedside light.

"Betsy?" she called softly.

"Is that you, Katherine?"

"Yes." Katherine lit the light.

Betsy squinted. "That's bright."

"Do you want me to turn it back off?"

"No. I'm not sleepy." She sat up in bed, her brown curls falling around her shoulders, reaching well past the top of her cotton nightgown. The little girl, with her flawless complexion and pink cheeks, reminded Katherine of a child in a fashion advertisement in a ladies' periodical.

"I just want to tell you something. Congratulations on taking honorable mention at the talent show."

"Thanks." Her tone betrayed her lack of enthusiasm.

"But there's something else. Guess what?"

"What?" Betsy perked up. She loved a mystery.

"Guess what we found?"

"The bracelet?"

"Yes! And the other things, too!"

Betsy clapped. "Where? Are you going to make me guess?"

"Not if you don't want to."

"Maybe a squirrel hid them in a tree."

"Close. Rover hid them in the yard."

"Rover?" She giggled. "Smart dog."

"Too smart, it seems. Apparently he was eager to get in the house because every time he did, he took something shiny."

"This means I was to blame, at least a little, then." She hung her head. "Are Mother and Father mad at me?"

"No, I don't think so. No one can watch the dog every second. But we all have to be more careful about letting him get into the house."

Betsy nodded.

"And Otis explained where you got that extra money. He said he was paying you to take letters to Miranda."

"He told you?"

"Yes."

"I'm surprised. He told me not to say anything." She hesitated and then blushed. "I—I hope you don't mind."

"No. Why should I?"

Betsy shrugged. "I guess I thought you two were sweet on each other. But then it looked to me like you think a lot more of Christopher than you ever did of Otis."

"I know you like Otis. Is that okay with you?"

"Sure. I like Christopher even more."

Katherine smiled. "I have to admit, I do feel better now that I understand the full picture of where you got your extra money. Thank you for forgiving me for even asking you if you could have taken anything that didn't belong to you."

"You're welcome. I always get blamed when something goes wrong."

"The plight of the youngest." Katherine chuckled and then hugged her sister. "Thank you for understanding. I promise to trust you always, from now on."

Betsy nodded. "Is Otis mad that you know about the letters?"

"No. I don't even know why he kept it a secret. We wouldn't have minded if he wrote to Miranda. But please don't keep secrets from us anymore. I'm sure that's what Mother will tell you once she finds out about this. Okay?"

Betsy nodded. The two sisters exchanged one last hug, and Katherine put out the light, wishing Betsy a good night and sweet dreams.

A moment later, Katherine joined the others.

"Is Betsy asleep?"

"Not yet. But she will be soon." Katherine took her place at the table.

"Christopher says you two stopped by Vera's," Mother noted. "She has some news?"

"I wouldn't tell her until you came back." Christopher pushed back his empty dessert plate.

"Yes, she does."

Mother leaned forward. "What's the news?"

"Alice delivered a little boy safely. Both of them are fine. His name is Paul Victor."

"What a lovely name. Maybe we should all have a second piece of pie in celebration."

"I'll take you up on that offer," Father said.

"Me, too," Christopher chimed in.

Father sent Katherine an approving look. Suddenly she was aware that no matter how many fishing trips he had taken with Otis, no one could ever replace Christopher in Father's heart.

"I think I've had quite enough excitement—and pie—for one night," Otis said. "Time for me to hit the hay."

Mother slid pieces of pie onto Father's and Christopher's dessert plates.

"With your permission, Mr. and Mrs. Jones, I'd like to take dessert with Katherine in the parlor."

"Why, of course," the parents agreed.

Mother smiled. "I'll be bringing in some lemonade in a moment."

Katherine couldn't see letting her mother wait on her hand and foot. "Don't trouble yourself. Let me."

"If you insist."

Katherine poured the refreshing sweet liquid into two clear glasses that had once belonged to her grandmother. Though Christopher was fond of dessert, she wondered why he wanted to take her in the parlor to enjoy it. The setting seemed so formal.

As they exited the kitchen, Katherine thought she caught

a glance exchanged between her parents. Did they know that something was about to happen? Katherine didn't dare think it to be so. She took in a breath.

Once they entered the parlor, she was glad Christopher had chosen such as setting. Though Katherine had been in the parlor often—mainly to dust it once a week—she looked at the room with fresh eyes that evening, perhaps because the night seemed to offer a new beginning.

Moments later, she and Christopher were settled into the sofa, as much as one could settle into unforgiving black silk cushions sewn with covered buttons and stuffed with rigid horsehair. As they partook of their pie, they recalled the evening's entertainment, reliving the highlights of their favorite acts.

"I think we can count this as a successful night," Christopher observed.

Katherine concealed her nervousness. Surely he hadn't summoned her here just to mull over the evening's events. "Too bad everyone couldn't win at the show," she managed.

"We all had fun, though."

Katherine finished the last of her lemonade. "I guess that's really what counts in the end." She sighed. "And to think, on this night, God brought a new life into the world."

Christopher nodded. "Each new life is a miracle, that's for sure."

They sat in companionable silence for a few moments.

Christopher broke the quiet. "Maybe this evening can be even more significant, with your consent."

She was glad she'd finished the lemonade. Otherwise, she might have been most unladylike and spit it out in surprise, certainly not an auspicious end to any evening. "Uh, what do you mean?" Time slowed for Katherine. Her heart beat faster, and her hearing became acute.

He set down his plate on the coffee table. "I have to admit, I was disappointed when I first learned Otis would be visiting."

"Really?"

"Yes. I was jealous. Especially after you and Miranda went to such lengths to impress him."

She felt a flush of chagrin. "And I tried to drag you along with me. I am truly sorry for that, Christopher. I will never ask you to do such a thing again. Not even for Miranda. But I think the trick with the horse was what clinched the relationship between her and Otis."

"If that was her plan, it certainly worked. Are you sorry?"

"No! I hope they live happily ever after."

"Just like in the fairy tales, huh?"

"Sort of like that."

"That's a good idea. I'll do the same."

"Are you still keeping our agreement to thank God for three blessings each day?" Katherine asked.

"I sure am. Tonight in my evening prayers I'm going to thank Him for the birth of Paul Victor, for the success of the talent show, and for you."

Katherine felt herself blush. "I'll do the same. Except I'll thank Him for you." Feeling perhaps she spoke too boldly, she continued, "And I'll add a fourth thanks. That we solved the mystery."

"Yes, that is something to be thankful for." Christopher cleared his throat and set down his plate. He drew closer to Katherine. "Enough about all of that. I have something else to ask you. Something I've been wanting to ask you for a long time. Something I had planned to inquire about before Otis entered the picture."

She felt her heart beating once again. "Oh?"

"You mean to say, you had no idea of my interest in you?"

"As a friend, yes." Her heart beat faster.

"Of course I value your friendship, and that relationship is a fine basis for my growing feelings for you. I suppose I'm not a man of great and flattering words like your friend Otis. I'm not as skilled in making my real feelings known." He swallowed. "I didn't want to ask for you to commit yourself to me while I was still in school, so I didn't plan to speak to your father until after I graduated. Then, when I came home, I discovered Otis was arriving in town and even staying at your house."

Katherine took in a breath. No wonder Christopher had been so distressed! "I never meant to cause you any concern."

"You know something? Now that all is said and done, I'm glad Otis visited. You've had a chance to sort out any romantic feelings you might have harbored for him, and he for you. You'll never have to look back and feel a trace of doubt."

She considered the wisdom of his words. "True. I know that Otis can never be more than an acquaintance. In fact, I doubt we'll resume our letter-writing relationship after this. Make no mistake. I'm not angry with him.

"Understood." Christopher let out a happy sigh, then took her hand in his.

She trembled in happiness at his touch. She found she couldn't speak, an unusual plight for her.

"Katherine, I'm hoping you'll allow me to ask your father if I may court you with the earnest intention of our future marriage."

She took in a breath. "By all means, don't delay! Ask him as soon as possible!" She looked into his blue eyes. "Not that there's any doubt as to what his answer will be. I know how fond he has always been of you."

"Really?"

"Really. I could tell he never was rooting for Otis."

Christopher chuckled. "That's good to hear." He stopped, returning her gaze. "I love you, Katherine. And believe in my heart, I always have."

"You know something? I believe in my heart I have always loved you, too. I just needed to come to my senses, that's all. At least I didn't have to fall off a horse like Miranda to see the light." She smiled.

"Please don't. I always want you to take care of your sweet self." He brought his face closer to hers.

Their lips met, the reality far exceeding the anticipation in joy.

epilogue

Finally, the day Katherine dreamed of so long had arrived. The day she would become Mrs. Christopher Bagley! To her eyes, the church had never appeared more beautiful, decorated as it was with fragrant summer flowers and lit with long tapered candles even though evening would not approach for hours.

Katherine watched her mother, dressed in a blue summer frock suited to the mother of the bride, begin her walk up the aisle, escorted by Ralph.

Katherine, knowing her turn would arrive soon, smoothed the white lace that decorated her white silk bodice. Vera had assured her repeatedly that the train kept its proper fall. Katherine dared not move too much lest she spoil the effect.

Katherine's first bridesmaid, a cousin from Virginia, took her turn walking up the aisle.

Katherine clasped her father's arm as she stood behind the church doors, ready to make her entrance for her walk down the aisle. Christopher would be waiting for her. She anticipated seeing the light in his eyes, knowing his expression of happiness would mirror her own.

Her second bridesmaid, another cousin, entered the sanctuary.

Katherine thought about their plans. Christopher had promised her a honeymoon trip to Washington, D.C. She hadn't been to the city since a family vacation years ago. She remembered feeling as though she was in the middle of a grand place. But to tour the city again with her beloved husband by her side; why, the thought was too delicious!

Her third bridesmaid, Lily, took her turn. The time drew near. Katherine could only think of Christopher. He would be her husband in a few moments. And she would be a wife. *Lord, I pray I will be a worthy wife for Christopher.*

Miranda and Otis, wed the previous month, were visiting from Charleston. When they had visited earlier, Katherine had seen the glow of love reflected on Miranda's face and Otis's as well. How happy she felt that they had wed and were there to witness her nuptials as well.

Katherine watched as Vera stepped through the doorway, taking her turn walking up the aisle. While her friend made a beautiful maid of honor, Katherine hoped that one day soon Vera would be a bride.

"Are you nervous?" Father whispered.

"No. Nothing else has felt so right."

Father's eyes misted.

She squeezed his hand. "Father, stop it, or you'll make me cry."

"I know you'll be living only three miles away, but you won't be my little girl anymore."

"You never need to worry, Father. Christopher will always take care of your little girl."

They exchanged a tender smile and then took the first steps that would lead to Katherine's new life.

A Letter To Our Readers

Dear Reader:
In order that we might better contribute to your reading
enjoyment, we would appreciate your taking a few minutes
to respond to the following questions. We welcome your
comments and read each form and letter we receive. When
completed, please return to the following:

Fiction Editor
Heartsong Presents
PO Box 719
Uhrichsville, Ohio 44683

1. Did you enjoy reading *The Ruse* by Tamela Hancock Murray?
   ❑ Very much! I would like to see more books by this author!
   ❑ Moderately. I would have enjoyed it more if

   _____

   _____

   _____

2. Are you a member of **Heartsong Presents**?   ❑ Yes   ❑ No
   If no, where did you purchase this book?_____

   _____

3. How would you rate, on a scale from 1 (poor) to 5 (superior),
   the cover design? _____

4. On a scale from 1 (poor) to 10 (superior), please rate the
   following elements.

   ____ Heroine   ____ Plot
   ____ Hero   ____ Inspirational theme
   ____ Setting   ____ Secondary characters

5. These characters were special because? _____

_____

_____

6. How has this book inspired your life? _____

_____

_____

7. What settings would you like to see covered in future
   Heartsong Presents books? _____

_____

_____

8. What are some inspirational themes you would like to see
   treated in future books? _____

_____

_____

9. Would you be interested in reading other **Heartsong
   Presents** titles? ☐ Yes ☐ No

10. Please check your age range:
    ☐ Under 18   ☐ 18-24
    ☐ 25-34   ☐ 35-45
    ☐ 46-55   ☐ Over 55

Name_____

Occupation _____

Address _____

City, State, Zip_____

Hearts♥ng